BLACKOUT IN PRECINCT PUERTO RICO

BLACKOUT IN
PRECINCT PUERTO RICO

STEVEN TORRES

MINOTAUR BOOKS

A THOMAS DUNNE BOOK ⚯ NEW YORK

A THOMAS DUNNE BOOK FOR MINOTAUR BOOKS.
An imprint of St. Martin's Publishing Group.

BLACKOUT IN PRECINCT PUERTO RICO. Copyright © 2010 by Steven Torres. All rights reserved. Printed in the United States of America. For information, address St. Martin's Press, 175 Fifth Avenue, New York, N.Y. 10010.

www.thomasdunnebooks.com
www.minotaurbooks.com

Library of Congress Cataloging-in-Publication Data

Torres, Steven.
Blackout in Precinct Puerto Rico / Steven Torres.—1st ed.
p. cm.
"A Thomas Dunne book."
ISBN 978-0-312-32113-0
1. Gonzalo, Luis (Fictitious character)—Fiction.   2. Sheriffs—Puerto
Rico—Fiction.   3. Teenage girls—Crimes against—Fiction.
4. Rape victims—Fiction.   I. Title.
PS3620.O59B63 2010
813'.6—dc22

2009041523

First Edition: April 2010

10 9 8 7 6 5 4 3 2 1

This effort is dedicated to
Damaris, who fills my heart to overflowing

and to

Beatrice Rose, our munchkin

ACKNOWLEDGMENTS

Many have inspired me to write this series about Puerto Rico—too many to acknowledge them all. I thank the people of Puerto Rico, especially my grandparents, Luz and Luis, and my aunts, uncles, cousins, and in-laws. I thank my sisters, Diana and Janette. I thank my most constant fans, Carmen and Esteban, my parents. You are all well-loved by me.

Among those who have encouraged me professionally are fellow writers such as S. J. Rozan, Michele Martinez, Con Lehane, Blake Crouch, Keith Raffel, and I. J. Parker. There have been many others— Daniel Hatadi, Russel McLean, and Bryon Quertermous among them.

One cannot forget the Jordans of *Crimespree Magazine.* Jennifer Jordan especially has supported my writing, and I thank her for that.

This book wouldn't exist without Marcia Markland. I don't think I'd be a writer at all if she hadn't said yes to my work.

ACKNOWLEDGMENTS

The difficulty with acknowledgments is that you cannot name everyone who should be named. The deserving invariably go neglected. That has happened here. If anyone reading this believes I owe them a debt of gratitude, I acknowledge that debt. You're not wrong.

BLACKOUT IN
PRECINCT PUERTO RICO

CHAPTER ONE

It wouldn't make a difference, but Luis Gonzalo tried hard to slip into bed without waking his wife, Mari. He'd been working till midnight and with paperwork and reporting to the officer relieving him, it was now past two in the morning.

"Some judge called," Mari said.

She didn't turn to him or open her eyes. If he asked her a bunch of questions, she'd wake up for good, her night would be ruined, and so would the next morning. Possibly the rest of the week.

"I wrote a note," she mumbled.

Gonzalo looked in the dark at the nightstand closest to his side of the bed. Nothing. He climbed back out of bed and went to the bureau at the far side of the room. Nothing. He turned to ask Mari where she'd left the note, but she was snoring lightly. Dead tired.

The note on the kitchen table was short: "Judge Eusebio Lopez. His chambers. Tomorrow. Eight A.M. Angry."

Gonzalo slumped into a chair, read the note over several times, and tired to think what Judge Lopez would be angry with him for. He hadn't had a case before that judge in a year or two. It had gone well.

He sighed. Being in San Juan at eight o'clock meant leaving the little town of Angustias at somewhere near six. It was only twenty miles if you drew a straight line on the map between the two cities, but there were no straight lines anywhere near Angustias in the mountains of Puerto Rico. Switchbacks and hairpin curves, yes. Straight lines, no. Twenty miles turned into fifty; and worse than that, much worse, was the enormous traffic jam that would most likely block the way. So bad, it had a name—*El tapon de Bayamon*. That could kill an hour just trying to get the last few miles into San Juan.

Gonzalo thought about going in to the precinct and making a few phone calls to at least seem prepared for meeting the judge, but that was silliness. His fellow sheriffs were all wiser than him and sleeping soundly.

It was close to three in the morning when Gonzalo got back into bed. He'd set the alarm for a few minutes before six. He'd leave without breakfast or a shower. This time Mari stayed in the land of dreams and rest. A minute later, Gonzalo joined her.

Gonzalo got to the judge's door a few minutes after eight. He'd forgotten to factor in time for finding a parking spot and had to run just to make it that late. He had a notepad and pen in his hand. He would jot down notes about whatever the judge wanted from him. Any reasonable man would know he hadn't had time to prepare in advance. At least, that was what he told himself.

He knocked and waited. Nothing. Another knock and a check of his watch. Okay, he was ten minutes late. That was substantial, but what purpose would it serve for a judge to call in a sheriff and then not wait even ten minutes? Like some juvenile game of "Gotcha."

Gonzalo slid into the bench next to the judge's office door and waited. Whatever else he did, Lopez eventually had to return to his chambers. Lawyers, bailiffs, judges, other sheriffs, criminals, victims, whole families rushed past Gonzalo as he waited. No one spared him more than a look. Certainly, no one was going to answer any questions.

By half past eight, the hallways had quieted a fraction. A little later, Judge Lopez rushed up to the doors of his office, a set of manilla folders under one arm, a briefcase under the other, a coffee in one hand and a set of keys in the other. He went straight to the door without looking at Gonzalo, got the key in, and balleted into the office without dropping anything. The door shut behind him.

A few minutes later, a lawyer Gonzalo had seen before but never worked with, went up to the door, briefcase in hand. The judge barked "Enter!" and the lawyer straightened his tie—already straight—put his hand on the doorknob, winked at Gonzalo, and went in.

Gonzalo tried listening at the door, but there was nothing to hear. It was back to waiting for a few minutes when another lawyer approached. Gonzalo hadn't worked with him either, but he knew the man by reputation. Something Marquez. Ambulance chaser. Good at what he did. For a second, Gonzalo tried to think of what accident cases there might have been recently in Angustias, but nothing came to mind, and then, from behind Marquez, another man emerged— clean cut, maybe forty, in a suit and a wrist cast. The face was familiar. The name wasn't coming to mind. They were admitted into the office without even knocking, as though the judge knew they were there without having to be told.

Then a stenographer. Young man with slicked-back hair ushered in by another young man, impeccably dressed—Lopez's court clerk.

Fifteen minutes of murmuring in the office and then the clerk opened the door to beckon Gonzalo without a word, just a finger wag like you might use for a child or dog. The same clerk pointed out a chair, and Gonzalo took it. The judge studied papers, flipping back and forth. It was five minutes before he sat back, adjusted his glasses, and brought his hands together. Gonzalo could tell the man was controlling his anger.

"You arrested Mr. Reynaldo Matos on the third of last month?" the judge asked.

The one thing Gonzalo wanted to do more than anything was to shoot another look at the man in the cast and match the name that he now remembered very well to the face that was only vaguely familiar. He controlled himself. The stenographer was waiting.

"I would have to consult my notes to be sure of the exact date," Gonzalo started. "But yes, I arrested a man by that name at the start of last month."

"A traffic incident?" the judge asked.

"I was called out because Mr. Matos had parked his car in the middle of the road and gone to sleep. It was on a curve. Very dangerous."

Judge Lopez nodded slowly, looked down at the papers again, shuffled through them, looked up, and readjusted the glasses. Lopez was bald with dark eyebrows and a dark mustache. His head looked a little too large for his body. The scowl on his face looked monumental, like a sneering pharaoh.

"And can you explain, Sheriff Gonzalo, how it is that with a simple traffic incident, the plaintiff here, Reynaldo Matos, had his wrist broken so severely that there are now three metal pins holding it together?"

Gonzalo knew exactly how the wrist was broken but the question confused him. He had written four pages, single-spaced at the time of the arrest he made, explaining everything. He assumed the judge had those pages in front of him in one of the files spread out on his desk.

"I broke it," Gonzalo started.

"Ah-ha!" the ambulance chaser said. He pointed an index finger at Gonzalo, then up at the ceiling as though he were reminding Gonzalo that God was watching everything.

"I broke it when Reynaldo Matos pointed a gun at me," Gonzalo finished.

"Oh," the ambulance chaser said. The deflation was visible.

"What?" Judge Lopez asked.

Gonzalo decided to tell the story from the top, just as he had done in his report.

"When I got out to where Matos had parked his car—on a curve in the panoramic highway, blocking an off ramp—his windows were fogged up. I couldn't see him too clearly. I knocked on the driver's side window, but that didn't wake him. Then I got out my baton and gave the window a couple more raps. Matos opened the door. I could smell alcohol, but I asked for license and registration. He leaned over to the glove compartment. At the same time, a delivery truck rounded the corner, almost hit me, blared his horn. I took my eyes off of Matos for a second to make sure I didn't get hit. When I looked back, Matos had his handgun, Smith and Wesson, .38, aimed right at my belly. I reacted and smacked it out of his hand with my baton."

Gonzalo was silent a minute. So was everyone else in the room. The judge closed his eyes a moment.

"I think that action saved my life," Gonzalo added.

The judge nodded.

"You're probably right," the judge said. "But why wasn't this in any report?"

Gonzalo fought the urge to shrug.

"I filed a four-page report detailing everything about the incident. I can produce my copy if it's needed, but—"

Judge Lopez waved him off. He turned to the other lawyer in the room.

"Serrano, what about this report?"

The lawyer looked ready to cry. He adjusted his tie, made it even tighter around his neck, and wiped sweat—maybe imaginary sweat—from his right temple.

"I . . . I only got the case a few days ago, and—"

"And you didn't have time to read four pages?"

"I . . . I thought the reason for the arrest . . . which is in the arrest report, of course . . . was not as important as the allegation of police brutality. You'll agree, won't you, that brutality cannot be tolerated."

"Of course," the judge said. "But who made the allegation of brutality?"

Serrano looked across the room at Reynaldo Matos and his cast.

Judge Lopez rolled his eyes about as far back as they could go, then turned to Gonzalo.

"You can go now, Sheriff Gonzalo. I hope this trip to San Juan hasn't been too much of an inconvenience. I must now waste valuable time instructing an assistant district attorney on the fine point of law that not every person who gets arrested and cries abuse is telling the truth."

Gonzalo stepped out of the office, and the last thing he heard as he closed the door behind him was the voice of the ambulance chaser saying, "How was I supposed to know?" and Mr. Matos asking, "I had a gun?"

The drive back to Angustias was almost soothing compared to the early-morning drive he'd taken. He took the curves of the hills easy, with the window rolled down and the breeze cooling him. It was ten in the morning. It wasn't his shift, but he decided to look in on the deputy holding down the fort—he was new to the job and young and Gonzalo thought it would be a nice gesture. As soon as he pulled the car near the station house, he cursed his luck. There was a crowd out in front. That might be good for a restaurant or bakery, but it could only be bad news for a police precinct.

"What happened?" Gonzalo asked no one in particular as he tried squeezing his way through the knot of Angustiados.

A little old man whose name he couldn't remember at the moment giggled at him, there was a scream from inside the station house, and Gonzalo entered.

The station house was so small that a glance told Gonzalo everything he needed to know. Past the three desks at the front were two cells with iron-bar gates and bare mattresses on narrow beds bolted to the concrete of the floor. In a corner of each cell, there were little metal commodes so low to the ground that anyone wanting to use them had to squat.

In front of one of the cells was the deputy, Hector Pareda, just twenty-one years old, handsome, but with an angry look and a hand on the butt of his sidearm. Inside the cell, Magda Herrera, a woman of about fifty though she passed for less, was sitting on the floor, sobbing.

"But why?" she shouted. "WHY? WHY? WHY?"

Gonzalo stopped himself from walking to the back and getting close to her. He could tell she'd had too much to drink. Hector looked at him, and Gonzalo waved his deputy over.

Hector came over, but he didn't look happy about it.

"She was walking in the street with no shoes on, cursing people," he said. "Drunk."

"And?"

"And I brought her in. Drunk and disorderly. She resisted." He pointed to his uniform shirt's torn pocket. "So I added that to the charges."

Magda now had the mattress off the bed and was trying to throw it, but there wasn't room in the cell for it to go anywhere. The cell had a small window to one side with bars over it. Someone's face was pressed up against the bars from the outside.

"This is a circus," Gonzalo said.

"What do you want me to do?"

"I want you to think. You and I have to live in this town and so does Magda. Her husband left her a couple years ago and now she drinks. To excess. Not every day, not every week. Maybe once a month. She doesn't drive or even own a car, but when she drinks, she gets a foul mouth. And sometimes she forgets her shoes—cursing and walking barefoot aren't illegal. Not even close. Essentially, you've arrested her for being drunk. Not acceptable."

"Public drunkenness is—" Hector started but Gonzalo cut him off.

"It's against the law. Sure. Fine. Are you really prepared to arrest everyone who gets tipsy in a public place? Christmas and New Year's are going to be pretty busy if that's what you're planning. Not to mention every Friday night. And Saturdays. And Sundays. And the weekdays."

"So I'm just going to let her go?"

"Well, first you'll calm her down, then you'll apologize, then you'll take her home."

"Apologize?"

"She's old enough to be your mother, Hector. Putting her behind bars . . . That has shamed her. You have shamed her. Think. How is she supposed to look her neighbors in the face now that you've made her drinking troubles official, public business? She had a problem. You took that problem to a whole new level. She's a lady. Treat her like one."

"Getting drunk isn't what a lady does," Hector muttered.

Gonzalo pulled him up short. "Then how about this: You're a gentleman. Act like one."

It took both officers several minutes to calm Magda and get her to stop screaming and abusing the mattress. When she was ready to listen, Gonzalo explained it all to her.

"My deputy thought you were lost and disoriented. Maybe due to illness. He brought you here so you could be in a safe place until you were ready to go home. I think you took it the wrong way and thought he was arresting you. He wasn't. Not at all. There's not a single shred of paperwork that says you were ever anything more than our guest."

This soothed her, even brought a smile to her face. She wiped away tears. When she was ready, Hector and Gonzalo both walked her to the only squad car and she sat in the front passenger seat as Hector drove off with her.

Gonzalo turned to the crowd and gave them the official explanation about his deputy's mistake and Doña Magda's understandable misunderstanding and overreaction. He wasn't sure anyone in the crowd believed him, but they all listened. If they went home to tell tales, they'd have to end with his explanation, and that was alright by him.

Gonzalo went into the station house to clean up the cell. She had thrown the roll of toilet paper into the commode, soaking it. He picked up one of her earrings and put it in his front shirt pocket. Then he picked up the mattress and put it back on its metal frame. As he gave it a final adjustment, he was scratched by a loose bit of its wire border poking out of the cloth sheathing.

"This day just gets better and better," he said to himself, and he was tempted to lie on that mattress and finally get some rest.

CHAPTER TWO

The plaza of Angustias was almost entirely original: a Roman Catholic church at one end more than 250 years old, a government building—*el alcaldía*—at the other end, with many of the homes of the first families—families and houses now mostly in decline for a century or more—lining the sides. But the plaza was at the top of a mountain, exposed to the full force of the tropical sun, and the trees that were supposed to give shade struggled for their survival, and the fountain at the center of it all rarely had enough pressure to provide more than a trickle instead of the jets it was designed to shoot toward the sky.

And nothing made it a comfortable place to be at noon on a hot day.

This is when Gonzalo finally left the station house and crossed the plaza, sun glaring up at him from the white stonework of the plaza.

Across the plaza and around a corner was his favorite diner, *Cafetin Lolita,* and he hoped it wouldn't be too full.

"Of course," he muttered to himself as he rounded the corner.

The diner was empty but closed for business. Lolita Gomez did what she liked with her restaurant, and if she felt it was too hot to cook for the lunch-hour crowd, she closed down and took a nap in the back until evening.

Gonzalo went back to his car and headed home hungry. There was a chance Mari had made lunch for him, though he hadn't called to ask. When he walked through the door, however, she was mopping, not cooking. She stopped long enough to let him enter, then asked, "And Julia?"

"Who?" Gonzalo said. He was headed for the kitchen because a sandwich could cure his hunger.

"What do you mean 'Who'?" Mari said to his back. "Your oldest child. Julia. The fifteen-year-old that got out of school early today."

"Oh no," Gonzalo said.

The thought crossed his mind to ask his wife to pick up their daughter, but he had made promises the day before about picking up both daughters, so he said nothing and just headed back out.

It wasn't a long drive to the high school, and he was glad his daughter was waiting for him and got into the car quickly. He needed a sandwich and a nap. His shift started at four in the afternoon, and since it was the Friday before spring break, he knew it would be a long night. Tired as he was, he remembered to be civil.

"How was your day?" he asked, pulling away from the school, but Julia was waving to a friend and didn't hear him.

He glanced across at his daughter, saw that her attention was elsewhere, and put his eyes back on the road.

If he had looked to his left, he might have noticed Luisa Ferré arguing with a young man. The man turned from her, she grabbed his arm, and he pulled violently away. She was in tears before Gonzalo had gone a hundred feet from the front of the school.

"Don't forget Lisa," Julia said.

"She's coming out early too?" Gonzalo asked.

Julia nodded, then reached for the car radio controls and put on a top-forty station and Queen was singing about the crazy little thing called love.

Lisa was fourteen and finishing the ninth grade at the local junior high school. Her last class let out at one in the afternoon and Gonzalo arrived two minutes early. Each class of the junior high school met in its own cinder-block building with corrugated zinc roofing. With bathrooms, cafeteria, and administration, there were six buildings altogether with grass in between stomped upon by a hundred students daily. Beyond the buildings there was grass six feet tall. Gonzalo knew that teens sometimes came onto the grounds at night to make out. There were patches of the tall grass matted down and every once in a while a lost piece of clothing was found. Gonzalo would be back that Friday after sundown, just like every Friday night, to shine his flashlight, make some noise, and make sure the kids knew they were being watched.

And he'd talk to the janitor who was supposed to keep that grass mowed. Not that anyone had ever complained about the goings-on there—he'd been sheriff for sixteen years and no one had ever said a word. There were no neighbors to disturb behind the school, just a cow field and beyond that a rank jungle that used to be an orange grove but hadn't been cultivated since he was a teenager himself.

The kids came out and Lisa was walking slowly. With a boy. She was smiling shyly and then she stopped and tossed her hair, and Gonzalo knew his daughter was flirting.

"That's Jorge," Julia said. "She likes him."

Gonzalo wanted to ask for the boy's last name, but bit his tongue. Mari probably knew all about this boy. He was tempted to get out of the car and shake Jorge's hand, let him know Lisa's father wasn't far away at all, but he feared making himself ridiculous.

The two teens lingered, talking, and as they talked, they leaned in closer to each other like there was a magnetism they didn't want to resist. They both laughed, then Jorge put his right hand on her left upper arm, and Gonzalo honked the horn. Lisa snapped out of the world of young love and into the world of waiting parents, said good-bye, walked a few steps, then turned again to wave. Jorge was smart enough to know he should be watching her until she was out of sight and smiled and waved. Gonzalo took a good look at the boy, tried to memorize his face.

"Is that José Arrellano's boy?" Gonzalo asked, fishing.

Lisa put her seat belt on.

"His father's Edgardo Belén," she answered.

That was all Gonzalo wanted to know. He tried asking how her day was, but she fell asleep with the Captain and Tenille singing about doing it one more time.

At home there was time for a sandwich, but even though he lay down, sleep wouldn't come to him, so he just counted the minutes until three-thirty, then rode off to the station house again to relieve Hector Pareda.

"Are you sure it's alright?" Hector asked. "I could postpone my vacation time. I could—"

Gonzalo put up a hand to stop him.

"You've done your probation time, you've earned your vacation."

"But right before spring break is probably not a good time. You'll be short-handed."

"We'll always be short-handed, and there will never be a 'good' time. Don't worry. Me and Collazo have been handling things here for more than ten years. Before that it was just me, and before me, there was nobody. Trust me. Things won't fall apart just because you're not here."

Hector looked troubled even after all the comforting. Police offi-cer was the only job he had ever wanted, and it was the only job that had offered him time off.

"Do you want me to take the squad car around town one more time? Show a little police presence?"

Gonzalo looked at his watch and shook his head.

"Nope. I want you to sign yourself out and go home. You've got a plane to catch and it takes an hour to get from here to the airport."

"It doesn't take me that long."

Gonzalo raised an eyebrow.

"Yeah, when you get back we'll talk about that."

"What?"

"Posted speed limits."

As soon as Hector was out, Gonzalo took a walk around the center of town just to show there was still a law enforcement officer on duty, but this wasn't the part of Angustias that gave trouble on Friday nights. The real trouble was on the outskirts of town and the more rural areas where fistfights could boil over with no one around to stop or report them.

"Looking for trouble?" more than one person asked.

He responded to each with a variation of "Are you making some?"

Back in the station house by a quarter to five, he got his first call.

"Juan Soto is drunk."

The caller was Mrs. Soto.

"It's not even five yet," Gonzalo tried.

"He's been drinking since noon."

"Is he at home?"

"Almost."

"What does *almost* mean?"

"It means he's sleeping in the gutter across the street."

Gonzalo gave in to the temptation to ask whether this was such a bad thing. After all, a drunken man could easily find worse places to sleep.

"His legs are stretched onto the road," Mrs. Soto said.

Gonzalo drove out and helped Soto get to his feet and then into a proper bed. As soon as he got back into the squad car, the mayor of the town got him on the radio telling him there was a fight underway at Colmado Ruiz.

Outside of the stores near the plaza, Colmado Ruiz was the most successful business in Angustias. A simple concrete and cinder-block construction, it was part grocery store, part fast-food place, part bar, and part billiard hall with two pool tables and four folding tables in case anyone wanted to eat a pulled pork sandwich or drink a beer while watching the lousy reception of the TV mounted on a shelf six feet off the ground. Raul Ruiz was a trunk of a man, round and wide. He ran the place and made good enough money from it, but it wasn't his charm or his business sense that kept the customers coming; it was the location at an intersection of two of the major roads of Angustias.

By the time Gonzalo got to the store, the fighting was over. One of the fighters sat with a bloody nose and a plastic cup of beer; the other fighter was laid out on his back on the ceramic tiles of the floor. His nose was bloodied as well.

Nobody seemed to notice that the sheriff had walked in.

"Anybody want to explain to me why Guillermo Salinas is stretched out on the floor?"

Ruiz spoke up from behind his counter. He pointed at the TV watcher.

"That guy there bumped into Salinas. Salinas spilled his drink, called him a few nasty names, and these two idiots started to fight. Real punches, too, not just pushing and wrestling. Anyway, I called your office, then the mayor's office, but they stopped on their own. Got tired of getting hurt, I think. And they bought each other a cup of beer."

Gonzalo thought about the story for a moment, wondering if he had missed something.

"So if the fight burned itself out, why is Salinas on the floor?"

"The spilled beer," Ruiz said. "He slipped in it."

Gonzalo worked for a few minutes getting Salinas awake and onto his feet. He helped the man out the door and didn't notice Francisco Ferré walking in and ordering his first beer of the night.

The sheriff took Salinas to the only clinic in Angustias, and Dr. Perez thanked him at the door once Salinas was in a wheelchair.

"I wasn't busy enough," the doctor said, and Gonzalo could not tell if it was sarcasm or a statement. A minute later, Salinas was out of his hands.

There was still sunlight available when Gonzalo got back to the station house, but not much of it. He wondered for a moment whether he could afford a nap in the station house, but another call came in, then another before he had gotten out of his chair to respond to the first one. By the time he had responded to these two it would be dark out and time to make continuous rounds throughout the length of Angustias.

CHAPTER THREE

At three o'clock in the morning, after patrolling Angustias for eleven hours, Luis Gonzalo finally drove to the front of his own house. He sat in the car for a minute, trying to think clearly of the duties he had performed that day, but he was tired in the extreme, and his thoughts slowly wandered and wouldn't fix themselves into anything resembling order. He was in the middle of nodding off when a car sped past the house. They were probably over the limit, but he said "free pass" to himself and got out of his car.

He had worked many late nights in his almost twenty years of policing, and he knew that the best way to enter the house without waking either his wife or their two daughters was to behave as he would have at three in the afternoon. He took care only that the doors he opened and closed did not slam especially loudly. Otherwise, he turned on lights, inspected the refrigerator, turned on the radio for sports scores and the next day's weather as he might have done at a more normal hour. When he was satisfied that the pie he wanted had in fact already been eaten and that his team had lost and that there would be a forty-second consecutive day of drought, he entered his bedroom and began preparing for bed.

Normally the nighttime ritual included unloading his gun and locking it away, but he was too tired for that on this night and his daughters were very nearly adults. He reasoned to himself that there could be no possible danger in leaving the gun on his nightstand. He unbuttoned his shirt in front of the dresser mirror and in the dim moonlighting of the room he examined his paunch. It wasn't extraordinarily large. There were many in town his age who would have considered themselves trim with double the paunch he had. He was sure he could still chase a suspect on foot, a short distance at least, if it ever came to that.

"Still," he thought as he roughly traced the outline of his abdomen, "*I* didn't hire a twenty-year-old deputy last year for nothing."

Then he thought he saw his wife's open eyes watching his self-examination in the mirror. He turned.

"Mari. Are you up?" he whispered.

If her eyes had been open, they were now closed. She gave him no response.

He finished disrobing, emptying his pockets onto the top of the dresser, and got into bed. She moved to snuggle against him, and he wondered if she did not move a little faster than a woman who was sound asleep should have. No difference. In their years together, she had seen him do many silly things before.

He lay awake. Mari never had that problem. She fell asleep quickly every night while he lay awake thinking. When they had first married it was something of a source of wonder to him that anyone could fall asleep so easily. In fact, he had often had to finish covering her with the blanket because she would fall asleep in the middle of that brief process. As she still reminded him with frequency, "The bed is only for two things. If we're not going to have sex, why should

I stay up? If you want to think, go to the library." For Gonzalo, how-ever, the bed, like the bathroom and the dining-room table, was an appropriate place to think. He had never been able to fall asleep without reviewing the day that had passed and planning the day to come.

On this particular night, with his mind given to disorderliness, he could only see the day that passed with melancholy. His patrol had once again taken him into every corner of the small town. He had once again said hello to almost every adult. Again, he had checked on every elderly or disabled person who could not come out of doors; he had gone on errands for several of them. He wondered how many times he had made the patrol and whether the town would not be better off if his young deputy took over altogether. In his years of service, there had been many arrests in town, crimes of passion, cow thefts, drunken fights, but there hadn't been an incident worthy of note in two years, and he wondered if the town did not waste its money and he waste his time by filling what certainly seemed like a useless role. A role Hector Pareda, his young deputy, would gladly and capably fill for less money. He himself might properly tend his farm for once and expand his program of reading and self-education. He decided that when Hector came back from his vacation he would go on one of his own. He would take four weeks and leave town. He would take the family to see New York or Washington, D.C., or maybe Paris once more. He would visit some of the world's great museums. He would add excitement to his life. He was being wasted in Angustias. "*I* have a mind," he told himself. "I should be using it," he thought, and in his drowsiness he added, "I should be solving the great crimes of the century." In his sleepy head he saw headlines that made no sense but which all bore his name, and he began to drift off into sleep though he had not planned the next day yet.

It is an ancient platitude that what one desires may be a danger-ous thing. If he had known the nature of the next crime to be com-mitted in his town, a crime in the process of being committed as he drifted off to sleep, and the manner in which he would solve it, he would never have wished for anything but the peace of the past two years to continue on to eternity. In only a few minutes after closing his eyes, he would find cause to love the boredom of the preceding years.

In the middle of the night, a minute after Gonzalo closed his eyes for the night, a scream was heard so loud, so terrible, so heart-rending, that, though it sounded as distant as if it were in entirely another town, Gonzalo jerked his body nearly out of bed altogether. He listened for a half-second and shot a glance at his wife, wanting to be sure that it wasn't just a nightmare, but she was sitting up staring at him with wide eyes. She opened her mouth and at that instant another scream was heard. The effect was again blood-chilling, but it sounded a bit closer.

Mari whispered urgently, "Go, go, go!" and, knowing what he had been thinking, she added, "It's real, it's real."

Gonzalo jumped out of bed, pulled up his pants, and slipped his feet into his shoes, no socks, in little more than a second. A third scream tore the night, and he ran for his bedroom door.

"Gun!" Mari said, and he came back to his night table and grabbed the gun belt. For an instant he was glad it hadn't been locked away, but a fourth scream cleared his mind of everything frivolous. Though still distant, the screams were definitely getting closer, he noticed. Also, they were definitely those of a young woman. He ran past his daughters, who were standing in the hallway in front of their rooms.

"What is it, Papi?" they asked.

He responded only by saying "Yeah" as he went out through the front door.

Once in the street there was little for him to do until he could identify the direction from which the screams came. His house was in the rural area that formed the outskirts of Angustias. There were only a few houses that he could see from where he stood, but lights were on in all of them. He began to hear shouts as his neighbors tried to get information from each other. The only neighbor he could see was his mother-in-law, who lived across the street and a hundred yards down the road. She was on her porch with a rifle. She looked his way. Another scream. He raised both his arms as a signal of despair. She waved her rifle farther down the road. The screams came from the valley. The valley he had patrolled a half-hour before.

Gonzalo ran down the hill as another scream was followed by audible sobs.

"¿Donde?" he shouted to his mother-in-law as he neared her. "Where?"

"En la curva," she shouted to him as he passed her. "At the curve."

With a few more steps he was able to see her ahead of him. He knew who it was. Luisa Ferré, a delicately beautiful high-school girl was walking slowly toward him from out of the depths of the valley. Her black hair was long and loose about her shoulders, but other than this she had no other covering. To Gonzalo at the moment it seemed as though she were vainly trying to cover her breast with her hand. In fact, later they would find she was scratching the skin off her chest.

With another hundred yards or so he would reach her. She let out another scream; he yelled to her, calling her name. Not heeding him, she left the road, cut through the tall grass at the edge of the pavement, and threw herself six feet into a rain creek that, due to the drought, was stone dry.

Gonzalo stopped abruptly, twisting his right ankle, and turned to tell his mother-in-law to call the station house. He saw her nod and continued running. He lowered himself into the creek and found Luisa lying there as she had fallen. Her eyes were open and she was sobbing silently. She was naked except for one white bobby sock. She lay on her right side, and even in the moonlight, Gonzalo could see she had many more bruises than could be accounted for by the short fall.

Gonzalo wanted to kneel beside her and hold her in his arms. His oldest daughter was in Luisa's class. But he restrained himself. To this day he has never been sure of his motives for not holding her. He would like to believe that he refrained out of an instinctual sensitivity, that he stayed his hand out of compassion for the girl's embarrassing situation. The thought creeps into his mind, however, that he was revolted by her situation, disgusted by her weakness, a shattered example of human frailty. That he was afraid to touch her and so saved himself the trouble. Perhaps neither is true. Deep pain inspires awe. Does not a mother grieving for a lost child awaken only a reverential muteness that borders on choking? Still, Gonzalo would have to live with the knowledge that humanity demanded of him that he hold that girl and that he disobeyed the strictures of humanity. Instead, he took off his undershirt and lay it across the girl's shoulders. A moment later his wife arrived.

"Do you have any clothes for this girl? Great."

Mari had taken off her own robe and proceeded to enfold Luisa in it and in her arms.

"Get the car," she told Gonzalo.

Gonzalo jogged back home. He rushed inside, ignoring his daughters, and got his keys and shirt. His daughters didn't even try to ask him any more questions as he rushed out again and got into his car.

As he began to pull out onto the street, his old deputy, Emilio Collazo, pulled up in front of the house.

"What's the problem?" he asked.

Gonzalo spoke softly to avoid being heard by his daughters inside.

"Do you know Luisa Ferré? It looks like she's been violated. I'm taking her to the clinic. Bring her parents, but if you see anyone suspicious in the valley bring them in. Period."

"People have rights," Collazo said, repeating one of the younger deputy's favorite phrases.

"Rights? Not tonight. Bastard's probably out of town already, but if not he'll wish he was. Your gun loaded?"

"Yup."

"Get to work."

Gonzalo drove his wife and Luisa to the town's clinic at as high a speed as he dared on a dark night. He and Mari walked Luisa into the building between them and put her in the care of the nurse, who was the only medical person on duty at that hour. They helped her onto a gurney, and the nurse wheeled the girl into a room, giving Gonzalo a look that warned him against following. Mari stayed with Luisa. She knew the girl better than her husband did, and she wanted to be there the moment Luisa wanted to talk.

"Go," she told her husband.

He had leaned up against the hallway wall, tilting his head back, blaming himself, not thinking clearly about the job ahead of him.

"Go," Mari said, and she put her hand on his arm. "You have work to do."

Gonzalo walked a few steps toward the door, then turned and stared up at the clinic ceiling.

"What are you doing?" Mari asked.

"I'm thinking!" he snapped. "I can't go out there without a plan. Give me half a chance, okay?"

Mari was hardly the one to be afraid of his little blowups.

"What is there to think about? Someone did this, and they have to pay for it. They were in the valley. Get out there and find them, that's all."

Gonzalo didn't hear her last few words; he was sprinting out of the clinic and into the night.

Gonzalo returned to his car in a hurry. He would make a quick patrol of the central part of town; then he would descend into the valley from which Luisa had walked, the same valley in which she lived. He was suspicious of everything, every car he could not immediately recall, every light on in the houses he passed. And he blamed himself for the attack. He had seen her earlier that night with friends and had sent them home, but he didn't escort them home. He had watched her leave the pasture they were having their party in, but he didn't watch her all the way to her house. That, he thought, made all the difference.

As he neared Luisa's house at the lowest point in the valley, he came across Collazo's car.

"Any arrests?"

"No."

"Did you get her parents? I forgot to tell you not to tell them anything about the attack until the nurse examined her."

"I didn't get her parents," Collazo said.

"Why not?"

"I think Ferré might have done it."

This information stunned Gonzalo to such a degree that he could only sit in his car in opened-mouth silence for a full minute until Collazo, sensing the awkwardness of the moment and his statement, continued.

"I left Ferré at midnight. He was drinking but not drunk. When I got to his house now, I tripped over him. He was sleeping on the porch, stone drunk. The knuckles on both hands are bloody now, but when I left him at twelve, he was fine. I decided to leave him until I heard from you."

Gonzalo paused for a moment. Bringing Francisco Ferré in, even for questioning, would be a drastic step. You didn't bring people in unless you were ready to ruin their reputations. Francisco Ferré didn't have the greatest reputation, but he was becoming a stable member of the community, and he wouldn't be anymore if he had to be brought in for this as a serious suspect even if he was eventually cleared. Collazo was certainly not the type to make so harsh an accusation without being fully convinced that the accusation was warranted. But if Ferré was unconscious, then he might just as well stay on his porch. Also, there was no point in arresting the girl's father without having heard from the nurse or the girl herself.

"Leave him on his porch. Go into town. Get the mayor and deputy mayor. Tell them to come down into the valley, armed. I'm going to be in the fields. Go to the clinic, find out how she is, was she raped. Ask Mari if she's talking. Let me see. It's three forty-five. Find me in the fields no later than five o'clock. Get moving. Remember. If they're suspicious, lock them up. Get to work."

"Okay, but you want the mayor in the fields? Why?"

"That girl had clothes on at two in the morning. She was naked at three. If we find the clothes, we find the crime scene."

Collazo did as he was told. The mayor and his deputy had already been telephoned by citizens of the valley about the screams. Rumors were beginning to circulate. Both men drove down into the valley as requested, but they decided to leave their guns at home.

On his way out of the center of town, Collazo visited the clinic as well. The doctor in the case would have found it difficult to break the sanctity of patient confidentiality without some court order or, at least, the parent's consent. The nurse, Irma Pagan, however, had informed Mari that the girl had indeed been raped. Semen had been found in her vagina, and there was some minor bleeding, but no more than might have been expected from a virgin during her first sexual encounter or from rough sex. The pubic area, including her upper inner thighs, was bruised on the surface as though she had been punched there several times. There would be no permanent damage to her sexual organs, but the rape had been brutal. She had been choked and punched so hard that the mark of knuckles was evident all over her body. She had broken her right wrist possibly from falling into the creek, but she also had two broken ribs on her left side. These coincided with what looked like a heel mark. Every physical injury was expected to heal.

"She's young," the nurse said. "She'll be alright."

No prognosis could be made yet about her mental state. She had been severely traumatized and now she was sedated; this was all that could be said with certainty. She hadn't yet said a single word.

There was some evidence that she had fought her attacker. She had tiny bits of flesh under the nails of both her hands. That one set of nails had scratched at her own bosom was clear, but the nails of the other hand had flesh that belonged to someone else. This someone else was most likely her attacker. That she had fought back was thought by both the nurse and the deputy to be a good omen about her mental state; it was assumed that it showed a strong will to survive.

On the other hand, the fact that she had scratched herself—in fact, there was more of her own skin than that of the other person—was disturbing to them. They thought it showed she was disgusted with herself. But that was only amateurish conjecture on their part. It is probable that even Luisa could not say what she was thinking as she dug into her own flesh. When asked days later, she said only that she didn't remember doing it.

Before leaving, Collazo checked on Luisa, who was asleep on one of the two beds in the clinic. He watched her from a distance until he could notice her slow breathing and the barely perceptible flutter of her bruised eyelids. As he watched her for those few minutes, he thought of the woman he had married when she was no more than Luisa's age and the granddaughter he had who was no more than Luisa's age, and he felt rise within him a righteous, youthful indignation. He hated the man who had done this thing to Luisa, and he vowed that this man would meet with justice. But even as he vowed this in his heart, he recognized in his mind that the administering of justice is never so easy, so simple as he would like it to be. In his years as Gonzalo's deputy, he had been spat on twice by criminals who walked away from their trials because of technicalities. Both still lived in Angustias and went about their daily business as though they had never done a thing wrong; as though a name misspelled on a warrant was the same as actual innocence. He knew the most out-rageous crimes went unpunished. Retribution is sometimes neither swift, nor sure. Sometimes retribution is not at all.

In his fury, Collazo focused his hatred on Luisa's father. After his dealings with Mr. Ferré the night before, he was convinced that the man had gotten himself drunk and directed his unspent energies against his daughter. In Collazo's mind it seemed clear that Francisco Ferré, drunk and angry, had vented foul violence upon his own daughter. But Collazo was wrong. Francisco Ferré did not rape his daughter, nor did he inflict any of her wounds. He had not seen his daughter since the morning before the attack when she left the house for school. Collazo had no way of knowing this, of course, and at this point in the investigation it was rational to keep Ferré in mind as a suspect.

As Collazo based his opinion of the case on his recollection of Ferré's disposition in the hours before the attack, we should review the actions of the previous night before joining Sheriff Gonzalo in the fields of the valley.

CHAPTER FOUR

Hector Pareda ended his shift at four in the afternoon that Friday and was soon on his way to the airport to start his two-week vacation visiting family in New York. There remained only two police officers in Angustias: Luis Gonzalo, the sheriff, and Emilio Collazo, his only other deputy, and they shared what was left of that Friday—Gonzalo starting officially at four and Collazo coming in at ten.

While Gonzalo had the higher rank, he assigned himself the harder of the shifts. He let himself be seen from noon to well past midnight, making sure the schools closed without incident—that the grade-schoolers got on their buses and the high-schoolers did not congregate too late—making sure the drunks got home without stopping to sleep on the highway, making sure the drag racers, who started their competitions at ten or so, kept from racing down the main roads of the town. This was the main police work of Angustias, a town of less than ten thousand.

Emilio Collazo, the deputy, was seventy years old. Luis had hired him ten years earlier (when Hector Pareda, the other deputy, was still in grade school) as a favor to a friend and to make use of a budget that had been mysteriously or mistakenly quadrupled by the state. Emilio was strong for his age (for any age, thought Luis) and tall. He measured a little over six feet in height. He had worked as a farmer since he was old enough to hold a machete; he considered the eight-hour-a-day job relaxing, something to do now that he was old. Even with this job, he still farmed much of his land. He owned seventeen acres. Collazo was dutiful, following orders to the letter if possible, and he was intelligent though mostly uneducated. Perhaps best of all, he was naturally silent so that not even his wife of fifty years could ever find from him who was arrested for drunkenness and fighting, or which couple was quarreling at three in the morning. One of his few jokes was about how he would have his entire property under the plow when he retired and feel active again.

Emilio Collazo reported to the station for work a few minutes before his shift started every night faithfully. Normally he would sleep in the station in case the phone rang, but usually it did not. He would awaken at five or so to be about the town when the farmers went to their fields.

This night was different. It was the first Friday night Luis and Emilio worked without Hector since he had joined the force two years before, and every Friday night had its problems; *Viernes Social,* it was called—Social Friday. Friday was the night when the young and unattached tried to become attached if only for the weekend. The town's only watering hole, a grocery store/bar/pool hall— Colmado Ruiz—stayed open late on Fridays and up to a half-dozen young men might throw parties at their parents' home that attracted teens and college-aged kids from surrounding towns. The most difficult part of Friday nights was trying to keep track of car parties. Five or six cars filled with young people might drive onto lonely back roads or into fields of tall grass. That the young would party, drink, fight, and make love on *Viernes Social* was to be expected. Doing all this in seclusion, however, might lead to serious trouble. Luis would help Emilio patrol for a few hours. By three, he knew, the beer would run dry and the energies would be spent and peace would reign in Angustias again.

"Do you want to go in separate cars, or should we go together?" Emilio asked.

"We should go together, but we'll take separate cars. We'll get done faster that way. There are four parties that I know of. First, I want you to go to Colmado Ruiz and show your face there, buy a soda or something."

"*I* don't drink soda."

"Fine. Buy a juice. Walk into the store and stay a few minutes, let them know you're there. Then go over to Quinones, Perez, and Santoni. They all have parties. Just drive by and ask how things are going, any trouble, and tell them you'll be back at two o'clock to make sure they don't drive drunk. I'll go into the valley and check on the Majozo house, they have a party. Are the Garcias still away? I'll check their house. *I'll* drive by the pastures on my way down to make sure there are no car parties. Got it? At two we'll go out again and get them all home."

Both officers went out that night in their own cars, a blue emergency light stuck to the dashboards. The town had an official squad car, but only Hector cared to use it. The car was a little too sporty for the older men, but Hector looked good in it, and he knew it; the bolder young ladies in town had told him.

As instructed, Emilio went first to Colmado Ruiz. There he made his presence known by pulling into the parking area in front of the store, shining his headlights onto the pool tables, and turning on his emergency light. Later, when Gonzalo tried to reconstruct all the events of that night, Emilio would be questioned as to why he didn't simply enter the establishment and order a juice as suggested. "I wasn't thirsty," he would reply.

After a minute or so of being blinded by the headlights, one of the patrons came out to ask what the problem was. It was Enrique Marrero, a twenty-five-year-old troublemaker, a *vago,* a lazy person who had never worked a day in his life and was still being supported by his elderly father's Social Security checks. Five or six men stood just inside the store, looking out the door to see what would be the outcome of the confrontation. They were ready to laugh at the expense of either of the two combatants.

"What's the matter?" Enrique asked, slurring his speech a bit.

"Just letting you know I am here," Emilio responded innocently.

"You don't have to shine your lights into the store," Enrique responded, beginning to wave the plastic cup of beer he had in his hand.

"We have rights, too, you know. We're not just drunks," he said, getting more excited. "We work," he said. "Our taxes pay your salary," he said, jabbing the index finger of his beer cup hand at Emilio, spilling his beer onto the car door.

At this, Emilio got out of his car and stood with crossed arms staring Enrique in the eye. After a moment's thought, Enrique began to back away, making conciliatory gestures with both hands, spilling the last of his beer. He stumbled and fell backwards and made no attempt to get up. At last the men inside the store were provided something to laugh at and they began to turn away.

Emilio returned to his car, and just as he began to reverse his way back onto the road, an empty beer cup landed on the road in front of his car. He stopped, saw who it was who threw the cup, and waved him over to the car.

The man leaned in through the passenger-side window.

"Get in," Emilio said.

The man complied, sitting familiarly in the front passenger seat, sticking his hand out the window to catch the cool night air.

"Don't you think you're too old to be drinking with those guys on a Friday night? They're all *solteros,* unattached. You're a married man."

The man next to him gave him a sidelong glance.

"You're old, Collazo, but you're not my father," he said.

Collazo's passenger, Francisco Ferré, was a little over fifty years of age and a little under six feet tall. He was robustly built with broad shoulders and large hands, but he was an invalid. He had been part of a Puerto Rican battalion sent by the United States to fight in the Korean War. In one three-day battle against the Chinese, North Korea's ally, his company had lost over seventy percent of its soldiers to injury and death. Francisco himself had been shot twice on the first day of battle and was taken off the field two days later when the battle was over. One shot had shattered his left kneecap. The knee never healed properly and so he walked with a distinct and painful limp. The second bullet broke his left elbow, tearing nerves and blood vessels that fed his hand. This deprivation cost him the ability to perform fine movements with his left hand; he could strike a man with that hand and knock him to the ground, but he could not keep a child from taking a slip of paper from his grasp.

He received a full disability pension from the government, and this was enough to supply his scant needs. Everyone in town knew, however, that his arm and leg injuries, as painful, as real, and as frightening as they were, were not his real disability. It wasn't a limp or a bad left hand that kept Francisco from finding some work; rather it was drinking that kept him from being useful.

Francisco had returned from hospitals in the States at the age of twenty-one. He promptly married and began a family. He farmed his three acres of land for extra money and was considered by all to be a model citizen until he had a dream some ten years after his return. He dreamed that he was young and in Korea. There was a cold, soft drizzle, and he was freezing in a foxhole alone. He heard the distinctive sounds of Chinese soldiers advancing by stealth, the rustle of wet leaves, the soft sucking sound of slipper-soled boots in mud, an occasional whisper. A Chinese soldier jumped into the foxhole with him and smiled. The fight was over really; if one soldier was in the foxhole, then a hundred were just outside of it. With his left hand he grabbed the Chinese throat, squeezing so hard the man lost his smile and began turning colors instantly. Within seconds he was being stabbed on all sides with bayonets by dozens of Chinese soldiers who screamed at him *"¡Papi, papi, papi! ¡No la mates, no la mates!"*— "Daddy, daddy, daddy! Don't kill her!"

Even after his twin eight-year-old boys pried his fingers from his wife's throat, even after she had forgiven him a thousand times that night, he could always hear the sounds from his dream. He could sometimes put aside the guilt he felt for his attack on his wife, but never for very long. For a time it was even rumored that he could only have sex with prostitutes because he felt relations with his wife would only soil her. This was not true. The birth of a girl child, Luisa Ferré, who looked just like him dispelled the last of the rumors a few years later.

Francisco's wife, Yolanda, was considered all but a saint by the people of Angustias, and had anyone dared to impugn her reputation in town, they would in all likelihood have met with violence at the hands of . . . well, of just about anyone in town. It was clear to all that Francisco and Yolanda had a normal, loving relationship, or as close to one as could be expected.

Still, while the guilt of that night might leave him for a time, the icy fear of his dream almost never did unless forcibly driven away. In the twenty years since that night, Francisco Ferré had returned to Korea a thousand times in nightmares. The only way to avoid the trip was to be tipsy when he got into bed. But even in getting drunk, Francisco had to be cautious. Too much drink and he became prone to violence. In twenty years he had spent over a dozen nights in Gonzalo's jail cell. In fact, years before, he had nearly broken Gonzalo's nose with a stiff left jab, a punch Gonzalo wasn't expecting because he knew Francisco to have a bad left arm. Collazo drove him home that night to insure that he didn't go beyond the tipsiness that he had already achieved.

"Aren't you ashamed to be with that group of kids at this hour?" Collazo preached that Friday night. "All they want is sex. You're too old to be running around with them."

"Who are you calling old? I'm fifty-one, not a hundred and one." Francisco said this slowly rolling his eyes to look at Collazo. "I can still satisfy a woman," he said. "I'm going to get a woman tonight," he said, grabbing his crotch. "Leave me here. The first woman I see is going to get lucky with me."

Collazo became a bit nervous hearing Francisco speak. As a strict Catholic he had little stomach for drunkenness and no stomach at all for lewd speech. He would have liked to have told Francisco to shut up and given him a rap on the lips with his knuckles, but that was not the way to treat a man of Francisco's age and troubles. Also, he felt embarrassed by his feelings. He did not want to appear prudish, so he joked.

"What if the first woman you see is ugly?" he asked.

"I'll do like I do when I catch a fish that's too small; throw her back. The first pretty girl I see," he said, grabbing his crotch again, "I'm taking her into the bushes and giving it to her."

"What if she doesn't want it?" Collazo asked, still trying to sound offhand.

At this Francisco punched the dashboard loudly, making Collazo jump in his seat.

"She better want it," he said.

At that moment they came up on the Santoni house, where there was a party going on. Francisco pointed out the window and said, "Leave me here. I want that one." He was pointing at a voluptuous teenager who was sitting on a fence in front of the house with her tightly jeaned buttocks favorably positioned for viewing from the road.

"Leave me here. I want her. I'll walk back," Francisco insisted as they drove past the Santoni house. Collazo drove faster.

When they reached Francisco's house deep in the valley, Collazo watched him cross the street, checking for drunkenness, but Ferré walked a straight line to his house, sat on the front steps, and pulled a cigarette from his shirt pocket.

"Be good," Collazo warned him, but Francisco was already think- ing of a bottle of rum he had in his living room. He waved Collazo away as though he were shooing a goat from a garden. He intended no rudeness, but he began to feel fear surrounding him, and he wanted nothing more than to lock himself out of his own house with nothing but his rum bottle, the cows of the field, the cold of the night air, and his nightmares to keep him company.

As soon as Collazo pulled away, Francisco crept into his own living room as quietly as he could and found the bottle of rum, Ron del Barrilito. Before he had stepped back into the night air, he'd had his first slug from the bottle, and he intended to finish the rest.

He got stone drunk that night and walked for an hour or so, drinking all the while, before returning to his home at a bit after two in the morning. Collazo found his hands bloodied and bruised be- cause he had run into an ox in a field more than a mile from his home and pummeled it though the ox really wanted no part of him. Fran- cisco turned back toward home when the ox head-butted him into a ditch and walked away.

The rest of Collazo's midnight patrol went smoothly except for one small incident. After dropping Ferré off, Collazo drove over to a house party being thrown at the Quinones home. The Quinones were the kind of parents who sacrificed themselves so their son could at- tend private schools and dress well, have a car, and throw Friday night parties. Julio was his parents' pride, though no one else could see any good qualities in him.

Julio was in an argument with another teenager when Collazo pulled up in front of the house. The boys were on the porch a few feet away from each other; each was being held back feebly by the arm of a friend, and they were straining toward each other, the tendons and veins in their necks bulging. Collazo stepped out of his car and heard the other teen yell *"¡Hijo de la gran puta!"* Child of the great whore.

At that moment Collazo was a few steps away and saw Julio lunge free from the arm restraining him. He pushed the other teen to the ground and sat on him. He raised and lowered his fist once, twice, and a third time before Collazo got to him, and he punched the teen again and again after freeing his arm from Collazo's hold. The deputy took out his night stick and gripped it in both hands, waiting for the fist to come up again. When it did, he batted it down.

Julio howled and jumped off the teen, holding his hand and hopping around on the porch, forgetting his opponent in the pain. The teen came at him from behind and landed a full-swing punch at the base of Julio's skull. Julio dropped straight to the ceramic tile floor like a sack of potatoes. The teen came over to Julio and raised his boot over the boy's head. Collazo knew what was coming, and he tried to stop it, swinging the baton at the boy's raised knee, hitting it hard, but the boy was angry. He regained his balance and stomped Julio's head into the floor as he had planned. He raised his foot again, but the deputy used two hands to jab the baton right below the ribs, and the teen took two steps backwards off the porch, then took a seat on the driveway. He held his gut with both hands and looked around himself lazily, surveying all the faces of his friends who were watching him. The boy was dazed, wondering when the air would come back into his lungs. Collazo walked over to help the boy up, and the boy looked up at the hand that was being offered to him and into Collazo's face. He would have taken the hand, but he was afraid to let go of the spot where the baton had been.

Julio's mother came out in her pink bathrobe at that moment. Her son was on all fours, shaking his head.

"¡Ay, ay, ay! ¡Mira lo que paso!" she yelled. "Look what happened." Her husband came out behind her.

"Arrest him!" she yelled, pointing at the other boy. "Julio's bleeding, Julio's bleeding! Arrest that boy!" she screamed when her son finally stood up.

"I can't arrest him unless I arrest Julio, too. They were both fighting. Julio swung first."

"But Julio's bleeding," the mother insisted.

Collazo took a close look. There was a tiny trickle of blood from a spot on Julio's cheekbone.

"That blood's from a pimple. It must have popped when he hit the ground. Look, if I arrest one, I have to arrest both. Do you want that? I didn't think so. Leave it alone then."

"Son." He turned to Julio. "Go inside, wash your face, and get to bed. You'll feel worse in the morning.

"Folks." He turned to the other teenagers still on the porch. "Go home, kids. This party is over. That's right. Go home.

"No party next week, okay?" He turned to Julio's mother.

Julio's mother let her jaw drop open.

"What kind of policing is that?" she asked, following Collazo to his car.

"It's the best I can do here."

"That's your best?" she asked as he buckled his seat belt.

"You're a lousy cop, Collazo. I'll talk to Gonzalo in the morning," she told him.

He shrugged and turned from her. He wanted to say something about her being a lousy mother, but he thought for a moment and held his tongue. It's not like the insult he had prepared for her would make her calm down and go back inside, which is what he really wanted. He got in his car and started to pull away from the house.

"You're not worth the four dollars an hour you get!" she yelled as he drove off.

The words about his pay stung him more than he knew they should have.

"What a woman," he whispered to himself as he drove along. He left unsaid the fact that he made twice what she thought he earned.

Collazo calmed himself before visiting the other parties, and he returned to the station house to wait for Gonzalo and the two o'clock patrol.

Gonzalo's midnight patrol also went fairly smoothly. He drove by the Majozo house, slowing down though even he wasn't sure why. The Friday night party at the Majozo house consisted always of the same four teenaged boys and no one else. The affair was too pathetic to be properly called a party. The boys were complete innocents who had known each other since before grade school; they'd begun meeting on Friday evenings when they reached high school two years earlier. At first, Gonzalo would stop to ask how they were doing. He did this to make sure they understood that their behavior was being monitored, that he took an active interest in them, but he soon stopped this practice. He quickly realized that these boys were absolutely harmless, drinking soda from plastic cups and eating cheese doodles and nacho chips carefully arranged in a "devil-may-care" attitude on a Styrofoam plate. These boys wanted no trouble, only gathering to talk about the events of their school week. Besides, the boys could never understand that Gonzalo was asking how they were more as a warning than out of real interest. No matter what tone he adopted, they always responded to his question seriously and at length. They told him of tests they had passed or failed, of soccer tryouts, and of new bicycles. They offered him Pepsi and invited him to sit. He only waved to them now as he passed on to the valley's lowest point, and they waved back, raising their soda cups. And for a few moments after he passed, they would recall how he used to stop and speak to them in "the old days," and each would wonder to himself why the sheriff no longer stopped, what they had done to offend.

Gonzalo continued on into the valley, passing the Garcia house, which was deserted. He entered an unlit part of the valley, pulled his car over to the side of the road, and turned off his headlights. He stepped away from his vehicle and, using a pair of binoculars, he searched the fields of the valley. He quickly spotted a group of lights only a few hundred yards farther down the road, evidence of cars parked off the road. He identified the farm as belonging to the former mayor, Martin Mendoza. Mendoza had so many hundreds of acres spread out throughout the valleys that he probably would not have recognized these as his own even in broad daylight. He was indifferent to his wealth, as indifferent as he had been of his mayoralty. Since he also was educated and an avid reader, Gonzalo considered him a friend, though Martin was indifferent to this as well.

Gonzalo put his car in neutral and slowly coasted down the hill, his lights off. He steered by the sight of the tall grass, never letting the car get too close to the edge of the highway. He parked in front of the gate the youths had opened to gain access to the field. From this position he could hear the teens laughing. He made out individual voices, but none that he recognized. Out-of-towners. He got out his flashlight and walked into the field.

"Hey! You kids aren't supposed to be here. This is a private farm. You're all trespassing."

He said this as he shone his flashlight from one face to the next. There were four cars and what seemed like eight couples. A few of them he recognized. Several of them held open beer cans, and, for a moment, they seemed startled. A leader stepped forward.

"Did you speak to the owner? If it's okay with him, it's not trespassing," he said.

"What are you? Some kind of lawyer?" Gonzalo replied. "Do you even know who the owner is?"

"You didn't answer my question," said the youth.

On occasion, Gonzalo could be provoked to argue even with a teenager, but he was determined that this was not going to be one of those occasions; the night had already been a long one, and there were some hours left to go before he got into bed.

"Okay, counselor. I'll go wake up the owner. If he didn't give you permission, I'm coming back to arrest you. You can stay in Angustias until Monday, when I take you to the judge in San Juan. Also, don't walk around too much in these fields. Eight hundred cows live here. Watch out for turds, they're even worse than the bulls."

Gonzalo left the teens with these two patent falsehoods. He had no intention of waking Martin to ask him about kids in a field that had not been used for cows or any other thing in years. His plan was to come back at two in the morning and force them out then if they were still there. He did not doubt, however, that he would find the field empty by then.

It was during this confrontation that he had first noticed Luisa Ferré that night. She was with one of the boys in the field, a long and ugly out-of-towner who, he would later find out, was named Carlos Romero. He knew that the mystery of school board zoning had placed her in a high school outside of Angustias; it had happened also to both his daughters. He was not surprised therefore that she should be dating someone from out of town. He thought, however, that he had seen a former boyfriend of hers in the field as well. That could be a source of trouble. He would ask his wife for future reference. The group seemed to be good-natured enough, so Gonzalo did not think that any trouble might arise on account of this former relationship. As the father of teen girls, he was getting himself used to the fact that teen relationships were transient even though he didn't remember his teenage years being like that.

When Gonzalo returned at two, he was surprised to find that none of the cars had left. In fact, two of the couples were in the tall grass and several out-of-town girls had joined the group though there were no extra cars. Now the group numbered about twenty, and several of the young men were clearly drunk. This time he shined his headlights directly onto the group, and when he got out of his car, he had his night stick in hand. He argued and threatened them with arrest to get them to consent to leave. He tested the drivers to make sure they could walk a straight line. Except for the two new girls who claimed to live not too far down the road, he herded the teens into their cars and watched them drive their separate ways. The two girls also he watched walk down off the hill. When he lost sight of the cars and the girls, he turned his car toward home.

It did not occur to him then that he had not seen Luisa or her boyfriend with the group this time.

CHAPTER FIVE

Gonzalo began his search by driving to the Ferré house. Like all mountain roads in Puerto Rico, the road on which the Ferré home had been built hardly had a hundred yards to it that ran straight. Gonzalo lived on the same road, and Martin Mendoza's fields were on it as well. Coming from Gonzalo's house, going deeper into the valley and closer to the next town, Comerio, the Ferré home was situated around one curve, perhaps four hundred yards farther than where Gonzalo had found Luisa. Mendoza's fields were about another thousand yards down the road. The entrance to those fields, however, was only a thousand yards away because the road looped around several other small farms. The road from Gonzalo's house to the entrance to Mendoza's field was a very rough, giant horseshoe. The road horseshoed again in the space of another mile going into Comerio.

Ferré's house was one of the nicer ones outside of the center of town, and, like Gonzalo's house, it was one of the few houses built alongside the road. Many homeowners built their houses at least a few dozen yards off the road. This allowed for privacy since these houses could not be seen through the dense foliage that was typical in the tropics even in a relatively arid spot like Angustias. This foliage kept the high-beam headlights from glaring into one's living room at night. More importantly, the distance from the road meant that drunk drivers going too fast through all those curves would not crash into your home as they had done seven times to Gonzalo's house. He had solved the problem by planting a row of palm trees and painting their trunks white to reduce the number of people who actually crashed into the building. Francisco Ferré had painted his entire house white, but he had never had the same problem as Gonzalo; his house was on the inside of the curve going uphill, and due to the sharp incline cars didn't have the power to speed by much in that direction. Drivers going downhill would have to cut across to the other side of the street to hit Ferré's house, and no one had done it in all the years he'd lived there.

Gonzalo's first job at the Ferré home was inspecting Francisco Ferré's person. He looked closely at Ferré's hands, noting that the middle knuckles were split as they would have been after a fistfight. He knew that this was hardly the first time Ferré had come home with his knuckles split; even sober, Ferré could be something of a brawler if he was given an occasion, and it didn't have to be much of an occasion. He'd once punched a man for saying Muhammad Ali wasn't the greatest boxer of all time.

Gonzalo noted that Ferré's face had the deep hue of habitual drunkenness but no cuts or bruises. He had no shoes on, nor were they to be found in the immediate vicinity, but, while his feet were relatively clean, his pants showed every indication that he had been in the woods or in tall grass. There were leaves of grass in the cuff of his pants and seed burrs stuck to the legs. Had he dragged his own daughter out into the woods?

Having dealt with Ferré some many times before made Gonzalo bold. He didn't want to wake him up just yet, but that didn't stop him from turning Ferré over onto his back. Ferré just breathed deeply once in response to the motion. His shirt was still buttoned, but his pants were only halfway zippered. The belt was entirely undone. Gonzalo searched Ferré's pockets, making a note of the only interesting item: a pocket knife. It seemed clean, but a closer examination might be useful. He opened Ferré's eyes, and at the time he felt certain he was looking into the eyes of a monster.

Gonzalo made several widening circles around the Ferré home. There were several small structures on the property near the house. He looked through the open door of an ancient latrine that hadn't been used in years, but it could not have been the site of a struggle; it would have tipped over and crumbled. He checked the lock on a shack used for cleaning, toasting, and grinding coffee, but it had a Master lock on it and when he lifted the lock to see if it would give, he disturbed the home of a dozen baby spiders, destroying their tiny webs. The door hadn't been opened in a week. Another shack a few feet away was open with screened windows, but inside there was only a hammock folded away on a shelf, apparently reserved for resting on the hottest summer days. Another tiny shack, attached to the back of the Ferré home, contained only a washer, a dryer, and room for nothing else. It was still too dark to navigate the Ferré farm, but he shined his flashlight into the woods around the house, slowly moving from tree to tree. He found no signs of struggle and no girl's clothing.

Back at the front of the house again, he found Ferré in the position he'd left him. There was a part of the sheriff, a loud voice working at the back of his mind, that wanted to put cuffs on Ferré on the spot. He wasn't positive Ferré had attacked his own daughter, but it certainly looked like he had attacked someone in the time since

Collazo dropped him off, and Luisa was the only victim Gonzalo knew of. Still, the evidence was circumstantial so far and Ferré wasn't likely to be going anywhere soon.

He decided to head for Mendoza's fields as he had told Collazo he would.

He entered Martin Mendoza's field through the same gate he had used just a few hours earlier. Mendoza's land was the best land in Angustias. This one field contained a hundred completely flat acres. The rest was so slightly inclined that if you were walking on the property, you would only be able to tell the difference when you started to breathe harder with each step. The hundred flat acres started in the area where the car party had been. The grass there was six feet high or so in many places, and the plateau had only a few trees to it. Each of the trees had been there for decades if not centuries, and the *flamboyán* trees with their bright red flowers, the mango trees, and the breadfruit trees gave excellent shade where they were found. If you didn't look up into the nearby mountains but focused on just the hundred acres, it might remind you of an African savannah.

Gonzalo thought of this every time he passed the property in the daytime. Now, as he walked onto the land, he was careful not to step on any of the footprints or tire tracks. There were cigarette butts and empty beer cans by the dozen. There was also a condom wrapper and a used condom in the tall grass. He felt certain that a closer examination would reveal more condoms and wrappers, more flattened-out areas of grass, but he was hampered by the darkness. He was in the field hoping to stumble across something important, anything, but in the back of his mind he knew it would most likely have to wait for the sun to peek out over the hills and into the valley.

A lot of things had obviously happened in Mendoza's field that night, but there was no sign of what he was looking for. There was no white sock or other clothing. He was not particularly surprised. The conviction was forming within him that Francisco Ferré was the guilty party, that the crime had been committed somewhere nearer to the Ferré home, perhaps even inside. For now he would just wait for the mayor to arrive so he could fully apprise him of the situation. He did not need to wait long.

"What's this about an attack, Gonzalo?"

It was in this manner that Mayor Ramirez greeted the sheriff. Rafael Ramirez was very short and extremely heavy. His arms stuck out somewhat from his sides like two handles. He had not brushed what remained of his hair, which was not uncommon, and he needed a shave, also not uncommon. In all of this, he was the opposite of Luis Gonzalo, his sheriff. Gonzalo was five-foot-nine, with broad shoulders, and he kept his mustache neat and his hair well-groomed. Since he had a very public job in town, he hid his natural reserve under a layer of gregariousness. Under pressure he might bark out his orders, but he was never thought of as rude. His appearance and his manner alike were thought of as gentle, graceful even. On the other hand, if Ramirez sounded something like an upset bulldog in addressing Gonzalo in this fashion, his appearance did nothing to betray this perception. He was normally gruff, and Gonzalo had learned from experience that when under pressure Mayor Ramirez could often cross from gruffness to unadulterated rudeness.

"What's this about the Ferré girl?" the mayor asked, ignoring Gonzalo's proffered hand.

"I found her naked a few hundred yards from my home. She was screaming around three in the morning. I know she was beat up bad. I think she was probably raped."

"So what are you doing sitting on your car in Mendoza's field?"

"I'm looking for the crime scene."

"Anything?"

"No."

"No clues, no suspects? Nothing?"

"Well, we have a suspect, but we have absolutely no evidence yet. . . ."

"Arrest him," was the mayor's response.

"It's Francisco Ferré," Gonzalo replied. Not even the mayor's heightened gruffness could easily overcome the shock he felt. He had no quick reply.

"What makes you think it was him?"

"Collazo took him home last night. He said he was sober and in good health. He's on his porch now, passed out. His knuckles are cracked like he's been hitting someone hard. I sent Luisa home last night from here at two. At three, she was screaming her way up the hill. Something happened between her getting home and her being naked in the street."

"Has the girl said anything?"

"Not that I know of. I have to check on her in the clinic."

"Good. Don't let her know you have a suspect; she might protect the bastard. Was she here with anybody last night? A boyfriend? Who dropped her off?"

"She was with an out-of-town guy. I'll find him," Gonzalo replied, though something entirely different was going through the back of his mind at the same time. He realized that he wasn't sure who had dropped Luisa off. He recalled clearly that she had not walked away from the field with the other girls. He insinuated from this that she had been a passenger in one of the cars. The driver might have taken her anywhere. At that moment it became crucial to speak to her boyfriend. He needed to confirm where they had gone. He refocused his attention on what the mayor was saying.

". . . And lock him up for drunk and disorderly, he's used to that. Talk to the girl; if she implicates anyone, go get them. Have Collazo get the out-of-towner. What do you think? Good plan?"

"Excellent. Can you lock up Ferré for me?"

"That's what I said. Weren't you listening?"

"Certainly. It's just been a long day. Sorry."

With this, the mayor and Gonzalo left the field to put their plan into effect. They drove to Ferré's house together. Collazo was waiting there already. He had not seen or heard anything to change his mind about Ferré; the image of Luisa in her bed served only to more deeply ingrain the conviction that Ferré was guilty. Still, though burning with anger, he calmly helped the mayor get Ferré into the back seat of his car.

Collazo explained to Gonzalo the extent of Luisa's injuries and told him of the discovery of semen in her vagina. He began to tell also of the lewd turn to Francisco Ferré's conversation from the night before, but the first rays of sunlight began to shine over the hills, and they decided it was best to leave the front of Ferré's house in case Yolanda Ferré, his wife, woke up. They did not know that she had seen the arrest of her husband by the mayor through a crack in her white, metal slat window. She heard none of the conversation and, while it was strange that the mayor should be driving her husband to jail, she knew that the process of getting him out of jail would only begin at nine o'clock when Gonzalo's normal business hours began. As it was only a little before five o'clock, she went back to bed. It did not occur to her that her daughter was anywhere but in her own bed at that hour.

Gonzalo heard the rest of Collazo's report in front of the town's clinic. The building itself was a fairly small, one-story construction with a check-in desk, a waiting room that also served as emergency room, two rooms with beds in them for the occasional patient who needed to stay the night and two offices and two examining rooms. The parking lot in front of the building was large enough to hold fifty cars and was surrounded by a chain-link fence. A rolling gate and speed bump protected the entrance.

Collazo's faithful rendition of Ferré's conversation from the night before did nothing but increase Gonzalo's suspicion. Francisco Ferré's guilt became all but a certainty to him.

"I think we have our man," he told his deputy. "I think we have our man, but I want you to find Luisa's boyfriend. I need details. I need enough to put a story together. Go to my house. Ask Julia if she knows who the guy is. He's from out of town. Probably from

Comerio. Remember, don't tell him what you want to talk to him about. I don't want any tainted information."

"Should I treat him like a suspect?" Collazo asked. In his mind the correct suspect was already under arrest.

"No, no. I think we have our suspect already. I just want to get as much free information as I can. If I can get something without telling him anything, better for me."

Gonzalo was only partially deceiving his deputy in saying this. In his heart he did believe that Francisco was the guilty one, but there was a lingering doubt. It was impossible to dispel the belief that Francisco had committed the crime. But it was also difficult to believe that a harmless drunk, never known to act maliciously, a person known to him for decades, would be capable of such a heinous outrage. How anyone could do such a thing, drunk or no, malicious or no, was inexplicable. Still, he reminded himself, there were the rumors of Ferré's dalliances with prostitutes; and men who went to prostitutes often enough harbored violence against women.

"We have to hurry. I might need you to track down a lot of other people in the next few hours. Everyone who was at Mendoza's field."

Gonzalo instructed Collazo about what to ask Luisa's boyfriend.

"Ask him when he left the car party, did he take Luisa home, did he argue with her, did he see Francisco last night. Maybe you should start by asking him to explain what he did last night. Just get him to tell you his story. Write down as many details as you can, tape it if he lets you. You got all that?"

"Yup," Collazo answered.

"Get going, then."

Collazo drove off, and Gonzalo entered the clinic to speak with his wife and the nurse and the doctor on call who had arrived at the clinic only a quarter of an hour after Gonzalo brought Luisa in. He estimated that the sedative Luisa had been given at a little past three would wear off at a little past six. Until then, Gonzalo decided he would wait in the clinic. He feared the contamination that might occur if the doctor tried talking to Luisa about her experience.

Like Collazo before him, he too stood at the door of Luisa's room for a minute and made vows about justice and vengeance. Making these vows had the same effect on him that it had had on Collazo; he felt anger and frustration and he focused his hatred on the prime suspect. In his mind, Francisco Ferré took on the shape of a sub-human monstrosity who could not be justly repaid for his deed even if all the rage and wrath of all the world were poured out upon him with no mercy and no quarter given. He looked to his wife, coming toward him from the nurse's office.

They sat on chairs in the hallway. She turned her eyes to him and in that moment there welled up within him such a feeling of . . . well, he couldn't really say precisely of what this feeling consisted, but it was strong. He moved to her side and vowed to her in whispers that no similar thing could ever happen to her or to their daughters while he lived. She looked upon his face with love and, cupping his chin in the palm of her hand, she said to him quietly, "You can't be everywhere."

Maybe it was the exhaustion talking. Maybe it was adrenaline. Gonzalo protested that he most certainly would be everywhere if that was what their defense required. He cried hot and bitter tears onto his wife's lap, and insisted that no prospective offender could be as staunchly determined in purpose or as fiercely savage in execution as he. But his tears and protests went for nothing. He knew his words were empty even as he spoke them. Evil would never consent to fight him on equal terms; and if it did, that was no guarantee of his being victorious. He recognized as he insisted and cried that he was not perfect, that he might invite evil into his own home without even being aware of it.

It was in this way that Gonzalo passed some of the time until Luisa awoke. When he could no longer bear sitting uselessly, when he had tired of his self-pity, he returned to the valley, searching with his flashlight for the crime scene, for clues, for anything that might help. He came back to the clinic after a fruitless hour.

While he cried and searched aimlessly, others were hard at work and did much. In fact, almost as soon as he was out of Gonzalo's line of sight, Mayor Ramirez made sure to brake sharply, causing Ferré to slide off the back seat and onto the floor of the car. While Ramirez had intended in this way to annoy his prisoner, he failed. Ferré had been propped up into his seat and, being still nearly unconscious from drink, made absolutely no protest about his rude transfer from cushion to carpet. In fact, he began to breathe heavily within a minute. Rather than injure Ferré, the move to the floor proved to be of some minor, short-term benefit: the farmers that the mayor passed as they went to their fields saw no prisoner. Ferré was thereby spared being the gossip of the town for a few hours.

The mayor drove quickly. Though the ascent from the valley required careful navigation around many sharp turns along a very steep hill, he was in front of the station house in little more than ten minutes. Some might think it difficult for one person to get a large man, one who has passed out from drinking, out of a car, across a sidewalk, and into a building, but Mayor Ramirez thought nothing of it. Normally brusque, he was at that moment furious. Having less respect for a man who abused his own daughter than for any sack of potatoes, he opened the passenger door and, locking Ferré's legs firmly under his arms, he dragged him out of the car, across the sidewalk, and into the building. The sound of Ferré's head hitting the pavement and the steps in front of the station house went unnoticed by the mayor. They did succeed in temporarily waking Ferré a bit.

"What'd I do, Ramirez?" he asked as he moved himself from the floor to the cot in the only cell in the prison.

"Are you sober?" the mayor asked, locking the cell.

Ferré thought about this for a while before answering.

"I don't think so."

"Then there's no point in us talking. Go to sleep."

After this, the mayor was about to leave the building and Ferré was about to take the mayor's advice, but the mayor turned to Ferré again, unable to let the man off so easily.

"Let me just say this: You did a bad thing last night. God will never forgive you," the mayor told him, stabbing an accusatory finger at him, trembling with rage.

"Oh my God," said Ferré with drunken fear and guilt.

"You did a wicked thing. You are less than a man. No, you are less than a human."

"Oh my God. What did I do?"

The mayor ignored him.

"Yolanda will never forgive you," the mayor said, and then, as though he were adding an even greater burden onto Ferré's shoulders, he added, "I will never forgive you."

Ferré sat up on his cot now and held his head in his hands.

"What did I do?" he begged the mayor. "What did I do? Did I hurt anyone?"

"Did you hurt anyone?" the mayor shouted, stunned by the question. "Did you hurt anyone? You don't remember? Ask anyone. Ask Yolanda. Ask the whole town. Ask God. Did you hurt anyone?" the mayor repeated.

"Did you hurt anyone? What do you think I dragged you here for? Exercise? Fun? Ask me again if you hurt anyone, you bastard. I'll show you hurt," said the little mayor, waving his arms excitedly.

Now Ferré looked at Ramirez imploringly, his eyes begging to be told the full story.

"Did you hurt anyone?" Ramirez said, now more quietly. "Look at your hands," the mayor said and walked away, leaving Ferré to contemplate his self.

Alone, Ferré inspected his hands. His palms seemed normal to him. The backs of his hands with their knuckles torn open, did not give him a complete story. His knuckles gave him enough only to enter into speculations about his guilt. He imagined an attack on his wife, or on his children. Possibly, he thought, he had attacked a neighbor or a neighbor's child. Perhaps he had killed a man. He speculated wildly in this way for a half-hour or more until, in his drunken guilt, he cried himself asleep.

CHAPTER SIX

The station house in Angustias is a hundred yards from the mayor's house, across the plaza, near the church. The houses along the side of the plaza were probably the most beautiful besides being among the oldest in Angustias. Except for a few reconstructions, they were originals built long before the American takeover in 1898, built, in fact, before America. Like the houses in Spain they were meant to copy, each house along the plaza was of two floors and had a balcony hanging off the second-floor windows. They were painted in pastels, and many had the original, imaginative tilework inside. Having been built on a corner lot, the mayor's house was one of the largest on the plaza. It featured a skylight and a small, indoor fountain with goldfish.

Ramirez headed straight home after locking up Francisco Ferré. As far as he was concerned, the town and all that was in it were under his personal care. It was routine for him to try to take over Gonzalo's investigations. It was just as routine for Gonzalo to circumvent the mayor's meddling by keeping him in the dark about as many cases as possible, by working quickly once the mayor found out about the case, and by ignoring the mayor's involvement whenever possible. Over the years there would be many occasions when, in the middle of a case, Gonzalo would simply not pick up his phone, or he would manage to be unavailable—on the road or in another town or in the fields—whenever he thought the mayor might be headed toward the station house. In a simple case, eluding the mayor and his bothersome directives might be half the fun of figuring out the criminal puzzle.

When a stabbing had occurred in Colmado Ruiz earlier that year, Gonzalo had gone about apprehending the suspect without bothering the mayor at all, though there were standing orders to contact him if there were ever a serious crime. Gonzalo woke his two deputies, Collazo and Hector Pareda, to help him search for the man who had slashed at the owner. The man was upset that it was closing time and had left Ruiz dripping blood from a gash on the left side of his lower abdomen. The officers finally found the man at sunrise; he had run from the store in a straight line through the woods for a quarter-mile before falling down and falling asleep. The investigation was opened and closed without having awakened the mayor or anyone else in town, and that's the way Gonzalo preferred it.

On this occasion, it was impossible to keep the mayor in the dark. A child was involved and that automatically meant Ramirez had to be notified. A crime against an adult was a terrible thing, but a crime against a child was an outrage against the entire community. Also, when Gonzalo first learned of the incident, he had little idea who his prime suspect would be. With a violent felon possibly still within the city limits, Gonzalo thought it would be wise to get word to the mayor, knowing that he would be sure to inform the citizens of Angustias. Had Gonzalo had even the slightest hint that it might be Francisco Ferré who was guilty, he would have let Ramirez sleep until the bustle of the town woke him long after sunrise.

For Ramirez, the first order of business after his talk with Gonzalo and securing the prisoner was to let as many people as possible know what a bastard Francisco Ferré was. For this purpose he called several key people in town, people he knew would spread the word and not be overly upset about being awakened so early on a Saturday morning. The town's Catholic priest (evangelical preachers were then making small inroads in Angustias), Arturo Perea, was called first. This was a matter of mere formality. Arturo Perea would never have passed on such information to another living soul, and he was sure to be upset at being awakened early. Still, though he would have liked to have slept until much later, he got out of bed at that hour and began praying earnestly for the girl, for the father, for the mother, for the town and its mayor, and for the investigators. He prayed also for himself. He knew that later, when the sun had fully arisen, he would have plenty to do consoling and counseling.

The next phone call was far more important to the mayor.

"*Ola*. Doña Lucinda? Is your husband home? Yes. I know what time . . . Oh, thank you."

Ramirez drummed his fingers on his desk, waiting for Doña Lucinda's husband to get to the phone. He heard a trip to the bathroom, the toilet seat raised and lowered, the toilet flushed. He heard Doña Lucinda's husband, Don Antonio Rios, the owner of the supermarket in Angustias, pick up the receiver and clear his throat several times before asking:

"Yes?"

"Rios? Look, something happened a couple of hours ago. . . ."

"I hope so."

"The Ferré girl . . . you know the Ferrés, right? Good. She was raped last night."

There was silence on the other end of the line. If there was any man in town to match the gruffness of the mayor, it was Antonio Rios, but he was speechless. This was stunning information. The sexual assault of a minor was so nearly unheard of in Angustias that it took everyone some time to comprehend the enormity of what had happened.

"Who . . . who did it?" Rios stumbled.

"Well . . . I really can't tell you."

"You don't know?"

"Well . . . I have an idea, but I shouldn't say, really."

"Then why'd you wake me for? If you were planning to keep me in the dark, you should have left me there sleeping."

"Okay, but . . . it was Francisco."

"Francisco? Which one? There are seven that I know of."

"Francisco Ferré."

Again there was silence on the other end of the line. It is quite possible that through the decades many men had taken sexual advantage of their children in Angustias, but in the history of the town only two fathers had been publicly accused of having abused their own children. The first man was accused by his wife *post mortem*. She had plunged a large kitchen knife through his breast bone so deep that the back edge of the blade became caught in his chest and the knife was impossible to remove. This was when Collazo was a small boy. The man was buried with the knife handle hack sawed off, the blade still inside him protruding slightly through his back. The other father bled to death after being castrated by a crowd. That was much more recent. There would be little the criminal justice system could do for Francisco Ferré once the people of Angustias got wind of his guilt.

"Are you sure?" Rios asked.

"Well, no. I'm not positive. But he's in jail now."

"There's that much evidence against him?"

"Well," the mayor said in an offended tone. "We haven't arrested him without evidence. Believe me. He's in jail for a reason."

"I see." Pause. "Well, how can I help?"

Antonio Rios was not the man to lead a lynch mob. That wasn't why the mayor phoned him, though he wouldn't have minded if that had been the case.

"Oh, we don't really need your help, exactly. I just thought that as one of the chief people in Angustias you ought to be aware of important things going on in town. I don't want you to hear this from some gossiper. As a businessman, you need accurate information about things, not rumors."

"I see."

"Well, I've got to make other calls. Bye."

The mayor hung up. Antonio Rios sat on his bed for a moment, trying to think whether he should do anything with the information he had. After a moment's thought, he realized he had nothing to do with the matter. He wasn't about to go to the station house as part of a mob. There didn't seem to be any need for him to become part of a posse; the culprit was in jail. The Ferré family was known to him, of course, like every other family in Angustias was known to him—they shopped in his supermarket. He might send a condolence card next week. He might give Yolanda Ferré a few free bags of groceries when her husband had been buried. (The idea that Francisco Ferré might live out the day didn't cross the businessman's mind.) Still, he couldn't see that he could do anything at the moment. He thought of himself as vital to the life of the town and believed the mayor's reason for calling.

He stretched himself back on his bed.

"What did Ramirez want?" his wife asked sleepily.

"It was about the Ferré girl."

"Luisa?"

"I guess."

"What about her?" With interest.

"Her father, Francisco, raped her last night."

"What?" Sitting up.

"They just arrested Francisco Ferré for raping his daughter. He's in jail now."

"Are you sure?"

"What? You think I'm making it up?" Offended. "Go over to

the station house and see. Ramirez said they have all the evidence they need. He did it."

Lucinda Rios got out of bed and put on a bathrobe to combat the chilling humidity of the early morning.

"Where are you going?" her husband asked.

"To the kitchen," she said.

"Oh, good. Bring me water," he asked.

"Sure."

Lucinda tightened the bathrobe sash and walked out of the room, closing the door behind her. Antonio forgot the water less than a minute after he asked for it, putting his head back onto his pillow and falling asleep. Lucinda forgot about the water even as she agreed to bring it. Her trip to the kitchen was in order to fulfill the mayor's true purpose. There was a phone there to call all her neighbors without bothering her husband. By the time he awoke two hours later, she had passed on the news to almost all the families who lived on the plaza—the most influential families in town. She had also notified several families who lived on the outskirts of town and in the valley. To all of the people she contacted, she gave the same breathless information.

"Honey, I can't talk long. I had to let you know the news. You know the Ferré family? From the valley. That's him, *el cojo*—the lame one—he attacked his daughter last night. Raped her. No, no. There are witnesses. Plenty of evidence. The mayor called. Almost killed the girl. She's hanging on in the clinic. She's young. No. He's in jail already. The monster. Gonzalo? No. Ramirez is in charge. Anyway, there was no investigation, he was caught red-handed. I know, honey. They should cut it off. Anyway. Bye, I gotta go."

Lucinda Rios repeated this type of conversation two dozen times that morning. This is what the mayor had in mind, and it worked perfectly. The people who listened to Lucinda Rios, wife of the supermarket owner, were the same people who might have hung up on Ramirez if he called them. They were the well-to-do of Angustias, people of some cachet. These included the clothing store owner, the two accountants living in town, the executives who worked in San Juan, and the hair stylist/leg waxer.

At the same time, the mayor busied himself with phoning those people who would listen to him—some of the farmers of the valley, some of the men who worked in construction when that type of work was available, the car mechanic who lived in the valley, the manager and assistant manager of Antonio Rios's supermarket, and Jacobo Gomez, the barber of Angustias. In all of these phone calls, the mayor was as coy with his information as he had been with Rios. Most of these people came to the same conclusion Lucinda Rios had reached—they ought to cut it off.

Sheriff Gonzalo would have disapproved of this spread of information. He would have tried to counteract it if he had thought of it. He forgot about the mayor's propensity toward gossip in his hurry to clear up the details of the night. Most of the phone calls made only a very slight difference in the outcome of the story. Two calls were especially important.

"Doña Carmen? This is the mayor calling."

"I know who you are."

"I'm sorry to call you at this hour . . ."

"What's wrong with this hour? I've had breakfast already."

"Well, I have news for you."

Silence on the other end of the line.

"You know the Ferré family?"

"They live a hundred feet from me, across the street. Of course I know them."

Doña Carmen was a little older than Collazo. Not quite old enough to be thought of as a matriarch, but old enough to know when she was being spoken to in a condescending manner. Old enough to know a slippery snake in the grass when she came across one, and she felt she came across one in Ramirez.

"Well, it looks like Francisco . . ." Dramatic pause.

"Francisco what?" she asked.

"I can't say it." Coyly.

Doña Carmen, with little patience for snakes, hung up the phone. The mayor called back seconds later and got to his point much more quickly.

"Francisco Ferré raped his daughter last night."

"Impossible."

"We have evidence."

"You're wrong."

"*I* didn't make the arrest; Gonzalo did."

Technically, the sheriff had ordered the arrest, and, unlike Ramirez, Doña Carmen trusted Gonzalo's judgment. Ramirez might easily jump to the wrong conclusion, but Gonzalo would not have charged Francisco Ferré with such a crime without rock solid evidence. Of course, Gonzalo had not charged Francisco Ferré with anything more than drunk and disorderly conduct yet, but the mayor was not going to be the one to clarify this point.

"Doña Carmen, when you see Yolanda, well, I was hoping you might be able to break it to her . . . gently. I would do it myself . . ."

"No, no," Doña Carmen said. "No, no. I'll tell her. Better me than you."

She hung up the phone and sat on her sofa weakly. She had known Francisco Ferré since, well, since always. This was going to be a hard morning.

When he had finished with this call, Ramirez made one other. He called the sheriff of Comerio. Sheriff Molina was about fifty years old. He had served in the Korean War and gone through hand-to-hand combat and liked it. He was built along the lines of a bull with muscular shoulders and neck. His arms looked like they were carved out of giant blocks of oak, and even his shaved bald head seemed to have muscles on it. His method of interrogation was simple and direct. He would come into the interrogation room unarmed, take the handcuffs off the prisoner, and let the suspect take the first swing. Woe to the prisoner who didn't put up a good fight and earn his respect. If they cringed or cried, they were bound to be beaten even after they went unconscious. Involving the sheriff of Comerio in an investigation ensured trouble. Besides favoring a method that Gonzalo didn't approve of, Sheriff Molina also felt that he outranked Gonzalo because he was older. The terrible thing was that Mayor Ramirez thought Molina's methods were more effective than Gonzalo's—after all, even if there was no conviction, the punishment had already been served—and he also had some sense that Molina outranked his sheriff. He admired Molina's bully ways and felt sometimes that even he was outranked by the sheriff of Comerio.

"Are you up, Molina?" Ramirez asked.

"Who is this?" Molina's voice told that he had definitely not been up.

"Me, Ramirez."

"Who?"

"Ramirez. From Angustias."

"I don't know anyone in Angustias." Molina hung up.

It only took Ramirez two more tries to get Molina to listen to him.

"Look, Molina. I'm the mayor of Angustias. Now you remember me?"

"Fat, little guy with arms sticking out the sides?"

"Well, I wouldn't . . ."

"What's up?"

"We need your help,"

"For what?"

Ramirez told him the details as far as he knew them.

"You want me to get answers out of this Ferré guy?" Molina asked. He was sitting up in bed by then, a lit cigarette in hand.

Ramirez thought this over.

"No. No, we need you to put men in the field to find the crime scene."

"Damn. You don't even know where it happened? Doesn't that Ferré guy live near us?"

"Yeah, a quarter of a mile from Comerio, I think."

"I'm telling you Ramos—"

"Ramirez."

"If this thing happened on our side of the border, even if it was just an inch into Comerio, I'm taking over everything."

"Well, Gonzalo—"

"Gonzalo? Gonzalo thinks police work is just asking questions until the criminal falls asleep. If this happened in my town, I'll take that suspect of yours and show him a world of pain he never knew about."

"Well, I think—"

"Keep your mouth shut, Ramos. I'm coming over there."

Ramirez heard the slam of the phone on the other end and gently put his receiver down. He was smiling the embarrassed smile of someone who had just been insulted by a person they're afraid of. He looked around the empty room he sat in, and his smile broadened.

"Now," he thought. "Now we have a real sheriff coming over. Now we can wrap this up neatly before Gonzalo knows what hit him."

It didn't take long before the results of the conversation with Molina became clear, but other conversations took place that night that were just as important.

CHAPTER SEVEN

For a long while after he had gone, there was little for Gonzalo's wife to do in the clinic. Luisa was sedated, and the doctor would have no new information until she was awake. Mari's job was to sit and wait. It was a job she had long since grown accustomed to. She could not spend the time perusing the usual magazines available in the clinic's waiting area. There was no use in even looking at them— she had been to the clinic several times in the past year and the magazines had been nearly memorized. She sat in Luisa's room, leaning to one side of her chair, throwing her leg over one of the armrests, her hair almost touching the floor.

She thought about the young girl before her. She had been to a car party a few hours earlier. Why? What was the point? To meet boys? To fall in love? It couldn't be thought of as true love. At best, what happened at a car party was a counterfeit of love. Since being with Gonzalo, Mari had known true love and the love found at a car party was only a poor imitation. Why settle for that? But then, she thought to herself, "maybe there is a romantic side of love that I am lucky to know. A side not everyone sees. A side girls like Luisa only hope for."

Esmeralda Gonzalo, Mari for short, had been the sheriff's wife for as long as he had been sheriff. Gonzalo had seen her on the first day of class in his first semester of college in the city of Mayaguez in western Puerto Rico. Actually, he had seen the calf of her leg that day; he didn't get to see the rest of her until the second day of class. The class was a basic English course, and, as such, it met first in a large, tiered lecture hall, then in a number of small discussion groups. In the lecture hall, the first day, Gonzalo was looking down when from the corner of his eye he noticed a perfectly rounded, deeply bronzed calf go by him on its way to a higher tier. As a serious young man, he did not immediately follow the path of that leg with his eyes. By the time he got around to taking a second look, the calf had apparently found a seat and was out of sight. He cursed his luck.

In the smaller discussion classroom the same calf was seated, early and with its twin. All of Esmeralda was there, in fact, and Gonzalo chose his seat strategically. The chair next to her was empty, but he rejected that option. He couldn't study her from that close a range. He chose a seat a row away from her and between her and the door. He could talk to her after class, before she left the room. He spent the entire hour and fifteen minutes studying everything about her—her hair, long and brown; her face, strong cheekbones, aquiline nose, full lips, sunned skin; her arms, thin and elegant with downy hair. By the end of class, not only had he ignored every word of the graduate assistant's love for the splendors of English, he also had not thought of a single thing to say to Esmeralda. She walked past his strategic position unmolested by him. The next week, he vowed, would be different.

The next week *was* different. She walked by him talking to another young man from class. A young man who had taken the seat next to her, asked her for a pencil, and then asked her for lunch. Gonzalo could think of no strategy to combat this subterfuge. It wasn't until the very last day of the semester, when he had already calculated he would be lucky to get even a C in the class, that he finally said something to her. She was walking out of the room with the young man (neither can recall his name now) when Gonzalo made use of his position and stood in their way. He stared at her a moment until the smile disappeared from her face and she paid attention to him. Her companion stood by her, tense.

"I have admired you all semester," Gonzalo said. "I think I love you."

The young man no one remembers now without some help sent his fist crashing into Gonzalo's jaw, knocking him down and out. Esmeralda walked away with the young man, but looked back at Gonzalo struggling to get to his hands and knees. She didn't love him then, but she knew she was more interested in him than in the man escorting her at the moment. For years, her mother would kid Gonzalo that Mari had been obtained at the cost of a punch.

Now Mari looked at the young girl before her and wondered: What price had Luisa paid her lover? Had she given up her virginity? Had she been beaten for her love? Was it possible that a rival for her boyfriend's attention had done this to her? Or did she have an old boyfriend who had found her at the car party and abused her for her infidelity? Each of these possible scenes passed before Mari's mind's eye. Each one began to play itself out; then the prospective lovers all tangled together—former boyfriends, present ones, rivals, and Luisa. Then Gonzalo was there flailing away with his night stick, and Collazo too. And her daughters and her. Then Mayor Ramirez threw himself onto the pile with an agility that he hadn't had since high school, if even then. Ramirez was the oddest addition to the fray, rolling around at the top of the pile, having no effect on any of the participants of the fracas until he was on top of her. He looked at her wild-eyed. His face took up the entire canvas of Mari's mind. He stared at her wildly, his little hair plastered in waves across his brow with sweat. "Ferré did it!" he whispered fiercely to her. "Ferré did it!" He shook her by the shoulders, and she woke up sweating.

In a blink, the face of the mayor reappeared. Mari saw him on the inside of her lids. His face was in a snarl, about to speak. "I know!" she said out loud, opening her eyes.

She looked to Luisa in her bed. The girl was beginning to struggle, though she was clearly still asleep. In sixteen years of being the sheriff's wife, Mari had often filled the role of official hand-holder, and that is what she did now, moving her chair to a place where she could pat the girl's hand and reassure her that the battles of the night that had passed were not to be replayed. She whispered to the girl and stroked her forehead, clearing her face of stray hairs.

"Shhh. Don't worry about anything," she whispered. "It's all over with."

Mari felt bad saying these things. She wasn't sure any of it was true. Other women had been raped in Angustias. Sadly, sometimes the attack was just the beginning of troubles. So much depended on who believed her story and how her family received her and how the prosecutor treated her, then the defense attorney and the judge, and the press, and who knew how many others.

Luisa only tossed her head, a pained expression on her sweaty face. Her struggles were ending. She moved her legs restlessly.

"Calm down, *hija*. It's all over. It's all . . . ."

"Carlos," the girl said.

Part of being a good hand-holder is listening. People who need their hands held often need to vent some frustrations or anger. They need to talk of their sadness, of their tragedy. As a sheriff's wife, however, Mari was almost a deputy. She knew that along with their frustrations and sadness, people needed to vent their guilt, to give away clues. They needed to tell the story.

"Dime, hija," Mari urged. "Tell me. Tell me all."

The sleeping girl tossed a bit more.

"Carlos. Help me."

Mari would certainly report this slipped phrase to her husband. She recognized, however, that in itself it didn't mean much. It could mean that Carlos was at the crime scene, and she had tried to get his help during the attack. It could also be just a dream.

"Carlos, help me," she said again. Then, "You bastard," from clenched teeth.

It was another half-hour, or a little after five-thirty, when Luisa's eyes fluttered open. Mari had rested her head on the edge of the girl's bed. She was still holding the warm hand, but sound asleep now. For Mari, five-thirty was a good time to wake up but only after a long, deep sleep. Mari awoke when Luisa tried to ease out of her hand. Her head felt heavy as she raised it, and she knew it would be days before she felt rested again.

Luisa spoke first.

"What am I doing here?"

"You went through an attack last night. Do you remember?"

Luisa clearly did remember. Tears welled in her eyes and she turned her face away. She nodded.

"Do you feel like talking?"

It was clear to Mari that this was the farthest thing from Luisa's mind. The question was asked more to prepare the girl for the fact that there were going to be questions, many questions, than for actual information-gathering.

"I don't want to talk," Luisa said, freeing her hand and wiping away a tear.

"Okay. That's okay. You just said something in your sleep. I wondered if it meant anything."

"What did I say in my sleep?" Luisa asked.

"It was probably nothing."

What?"

"'Carlos, help me. You bastard.'" Mari mimicked the girl, including the pause between phrases. "Isn't Carlos your boyfriend?"

This was a useful line of inquiry. The girl had flinched to hear her own words. She turned away again at the question. This reaction promised much. There was some possibility that Carlos had something to do with the attack. At the least, he might have some useful testimony. She would urge Gonzalo to question the boy. In fact, if there were any bruises on the boy, she would say Carlos was the guilty one. At this point, Mari thought it would be good news to be able to suggest that anyone else, anyone other than the girl's own father, was the rapist.

"Leave me alone," Luisa said. "I don't have anything to say."

"But what about Carlos?"

Luisa looked into Mari's eyes.

"What about Carlos? Carlos didn't do anything last night. I swear to you."

Mari had nothing to say to this rebuttal. Nothing was more probable at the moment than that her husband and Collazo were right, that Francisco Ferré had attacked his own daughter, and Carlos was nowhere near. What the girl had said in her dreams was just that, what she had said during her dreams, not a reflection of reality.

"Leave me, okay?" Luisa said.

"Okay." Mari got up to go. "I'll send the doctor in. He'll want to see you."

Mari lingered at the doorway.

"The sheriff will be in to see you later, you know. Everyone wants to help, Luisa. We're on your side. Anyway, if you want to talk, I'll be in the hallway."

She couldn't bring herself to leave the room.

"Luisa. Could you just answer one question? Not about the . . . incident."

Luisa looked her way.

"Why? Luisa. Why did you go to the car party? What was there for you?"

Luisa turned red and her lower lip trembled.

"I went for Carlos," she said. "I love him."

Mari nodded in understanding and went out into the hallway. She found the nurse at her desk. "Where's the doctor?" she asked.

"Asleep in the examining room. He's not usually here until eight o'clock. How's the girl?"

"She's up. She can talk . . ."

"But she doesn't want to," the nurse said. "I know. That's the way it is ninety percent of the time."

"You've dealt with rapes before?"

"Are you kidding me? I worked in New York four years, in San Juan for three years. I dealt with dozens of rape cases. That's why I moved back to Angustias. I thought I would get away from that type of crime. But it happens here too."

"I know," Mari said. "Well, at least not as often as it does in San Juan."

San Juan was only behind New York in wickedness to most Angustiados.

"Who says? This is the third sexual assault this year."

"Impossible," Mari reacted.

"Impossible? Look, women here don't report it. They don't even know that their husbands can't force them to have sex. I can't name names, but I have a little file of women who have all the signs of having been forced to have sex. More than a dozen. Most of them several times. *Cortejas,* too. Mistresses. Several a year, every year I've been here. None of them want to talk to your husband. Most come when the doctor isn't around. They want to be treated by me."

Mari had nothing to say to all of this.

"This town should wake up," the nurse continued.

"And Comerio, too. Some of their women have come all the way up here."

"Do any of our women go to Comerio? Do any of them go to other towns?" Mari asked.

"That I can't say. Don't know."

"Are you sure about all this?"

"How can I be wrong about a rape?" Nurse Pagan replied. "Another thing. I'll bet you can't guess how many women in Angustias have syphilis."

"Syphilis?"

"The men travel to other towns. They have ten dollars in their pocket and they meet a pretty woman in a bar. They come back and their women get the infection. It's sad. Syphilis can kill women if they don't get treated in time."

"Syphilis can kill?"

"Sure. This town buried a woman last year. . . . No. Two years ago. Died of Syphilis. Another one has dementia; she'll be dead soon. A lady from Comerio, the same thing. Nothing to do but watch them die."

"But what about penicillin?"

"Penicillin? Sure. Some of the men go out of town and get it. Ponce, mostly. They don't come to me. The women don't come here or go to Ponce. They don't know what symptoms to look for. Even if they did know, they're usually too ashamed or afraid to seek treatment. Once they let it go too far, there's nothing penicillin can do for them."

At this point they walked into the clinic, and the nurse raised an eyebrow to let Mari know the conversation was over. Mari turned and greeted her husband.

"Anything?" she asked.

Gonzalo shook his head.

"Well, she woke up a couple of minutes ago," Mari said. "She only mentioned that her boyfriend, Carlos, had nothing to do with it, but—"

"Collazo's trying to figure out who the boy is. Did she give a last name? A town?"

It was Mari's turn to shake her head.

"Well, I'll look in on her. Maybe a badge, a gun, and a mustache will make her want to open up to me."

His smile was weak and Mari thought to herself that even when their children were newborns crying in the night, her husband had never looked so tired.

Gonzalo walked off, and the doctor walked in a half-minute later, yawning. Doctor Perez had only been out of medical school for a few years, and he hadn't been born in Angustias, but he had made the decision to stay. He was tall and thin with glasses and thinning hair pushed back in a DA cut. He took a chart off the nurse's desk.

"I'm going to check on the girl."

Luisa had fallen back to sleep, and Gonzalo was now standing in her doorway watching her breathe gently. The doctor went in and stood at the foot of the bed, reading the chart for several minutes. He looked up and back at Gonzalo, raised an eyebrow, and Gonzalo knew he wasn't wanted. He went back and found his wife sitting in the waiting area—ten folding chairs and a coffee table with ancient magazines.

"Want to go over what she told you?" he asked, slumping into the chair next to her.

In two minutes' time, Mari told Gonzalo all she and Luisa had said. It wasn't much. In the end, Mari was inclined to believe Gonzalo and Collazo had come up with the right solution to the puzzle. Luisa still loved Carlos, and in Mari's mind that pointed to someone else as the attacker. The nurse's words made it clear that Francisco Ferré might have been the attacker no matter how outrageous the proposition seemed. It didn't seem appropriate at that time to tell him of any of the other matters she had discussed with the nurse.

The doctor walked out of Luisa's room, and Gonzalo waved him over.

"Has she said anything, doctor?"

Dr. Perez rolled his eyes and sighed. He didn't like discussing his patients with people who weren't related to them. He'd explained this to Gonzalo before. This time, however, there wasn't anything to discuss.

"No," he said. "She's still pretty heavily sedated."

"Is there any way she could be woken up just for a few minutes?"

"You mean like in the movies?"

Gonzalo nodded.

"No."

The doctor waited for a moment, but Gonzalo didn't have a response, so he walked away. Gonzalo leaned back in his seat and would have liked to close his eyes, but he knew that if he closed them, it would be difficult to open them again anytime soon.

"I should head back out," he said to Mari. "Spin my wheels some more."

Mari patted his hand.

"You probably have the right guy already," Mari said.

"Yeah? You know something I don't know?"

"I know a lot of things you don't know," she said, smiling. Then the smile faded. "No," she said.

Gonzalo went out to the parking lot and was about to get in his car when Collazo pulled onto the lot.

"Anything?" Gonzalo asked.

"Yep," Collazo said. "I talked with her boyfriend."

"How did it go?"

"Not good."

CHAPTER EIGHT

Julia and Lisa Gonzalo had been born into a family where the father was the town sheriff. This meant that in all their childhood mischiefs, in all their adolescent struggles for independence, they could expect absolutely no leniency. They were often treated as little more than extensions of their father, and they were expected to behave that way. At first, this may sound like an impossibly repressive environment in which to grow. Nowadays, and especially in metropolitan settings, there is a feeling that children should be given freer rein, a wider berth, in running their lives. But adolescence is difficult; decisions are often required about issues the child has never faced before. Julia and Lisa did sometimes chafe under the firm guidance provided by both Luis and, more especially, Mari, but the high standards were appreciated by the girls. They were grateful for the character-molding their parents performed. Or at least, their parents told them they would be once they both had children of their own.

Still, though Julia and Lisa were the best-behaved girls in town and both very intelligent (Julia excelled academically, maintaining a perfect record), Collazo was always very nervous about talking with them. With them, he became as self-conscious as a schoolboy. Perhaps their beauty made him feel awkward, but then theirs was a beauty of youth and character more than of physical attributes. Aside from their parents, no one would have argued that they ranked with the top beauties of the town. Collazo himself suggested that they reminded him of someone he had known as a youth, but he could never say who that someone was. In any event, he felt this uneasiness when he knocked on the Gonzalo door at around five-thirty in the morning and Lisa opened it.

"You're not in high school, are you?" he asked her instead of saying hello.

"No. You want Julia. I'll wake her."

"She's asleep?" he asked. Lisa couldn't think of an appropriate reply. She left Collazo at the door and returned with Julia a minute later.

"Do you know Luisa Ferré?"

"Is she the one who was screaming last night?"

"Does she have a boyfriend?"

"Yes. Was she the one screaming?"

"What's his name?"

"Romero, Carlos, I think. Was she screaming?"

"Is he from Comerio?"

"Is he in trouble? Did he do anything to her?"

"Comerio?"

"Yes. Why?"

"Do you know his address?"

"No."

"Sure?"

"Yes. Did he hurt her?"

"Bye."

With that, Collazo returned to his car and drove away toward

Comerio. Julia was left at the door to roll her eyes as far back in their sockets as they would go.

"What do you think happened?" she asked her sister.

"It's better not to think about it."

"What do you mean, 'Don't think about it'? Maybe he beat her up."

"Maybe he did. Maybe he raped her. It's better not to think about it. What if you think up something wild about him and her, and nothing really happened? How would you look him in the eye on Monday?"

"I never look him in the eye," Julia replied. "He's stuck up. He's got a couple of girlfriends that Luisa doesn't know about. I don't think I could think much less of him than I do now."

"Why didn't you tell Luisa if you think he has another girlfriend?"

"I told her already. More than a month ago. She hasn't spoken to me since. She's in love. She thinks she's in love. Anyway, he couldn't have raped her; they have sex every week. He comes in on *Viernes Social*. She's been on the pill since last semester," Julia said.

Then she thought of something.

"What if she forgot to take the pill one day and got pregnant? If she found out last night, maybe that's why she was screaming. Maybe she went crazy." She looked at her sister wide-eyed.

"Don't even think about it. That's a big maybe. Just go back to sleep and wait for dad to come home, okay?"

"Should I tell *papi*?"

"Tell him what? All you have are theories. Besides, if she's pregnant, that's not against the law, and if they're having sex, or if he has twenty girlfriends, that's not against the law either. Just keep your mouth shut unless someone asks you, okay?"

The first thing Collazo did upon arriving in Comerio was visit the precinct there. Comerio was a larger town than Angustias, and so they had several deputies working each shift. There were only two on duty during the graveyard shift, however, and only one was actually in the office when Collazo came in. This deputy was only nineteen and had all the hubris that youth, a badge, and a gun could instill. When Collazo walked in, it never occurred to the young deputy that he might be talking with a colleague. Instead, he took Collazo's khaki uniform to be the work clothes of a farmer. Collazo's hat and gun belt were in his car, and he didn't wear a badge on his shirt, so the deputy might be forgiven; but perhaps he should have noticed Collazo's polished black shoes and the stripe running down the side of his pants. Had he recognized Collazo for a police officer, he would have asked what Collazo wanted with the Romeros, he would have helped with the investigation and accompanied him to the Romero home. Instead, he just looked up from his desk a bit drowsily and pointed southwards when asked where the Romero family lived. "Route 418, quarter of a kilometer, bright pink, cement house, can't miss it."

Collazo found the house easily. The Romero home was small; there were auto parts and a rusting chassis in front and a yard of gravel piled on the side. Spread out behind the house, Collazo could see the family farm. This was well kept if nothing else about the house was. From what he could see of the fencing and from where the vegetation began to run wild, Collazo estimated that the Romeros had seven or eight acres under their care; that meant they were full-time farmers and probably up already if not actually in the field. A light shining in one of the side windows confirmed this to Collazo. This time Collazo put on his hat and went to the front door, which was opened by a man of about fifty as he was about to knock.

"Can I help you?"

"Yes. I need to speak to Carlos Romero."

"That's me," replied the man with some trepidation.

He was short, balding, needed a shave, and had on clothes in need of washing. Even in the dark of night, it was impossible to mistake him for anything resembling a high-school student.

"Do you have a son by the same name?"

"Did that bastard do anything wrong?" the man asked. Without waiting for a reply, he strode toward one of the back rooms and began pounding on the door.

Carlos Romero, Jr., was a bastard in both the literal and the figurative sense of the word. His stepfather had married his mother when junior was about ten years old and gave his last name to her son. The mother, who had never been exactly sure who Carlos's father was, walked out with another man about a year later. She left the child to the farmer, took what little money he had, and was never heard from again. On the other hand, Carlos junior, who was now twenty and still in high school, seemed to threaten never to leave home. The senior Carlos had gotten him a job when junior was sixteen, but Carlos promptly quit. His employer had had the audacity to ask him to do something, and Carlos refused to be a slave, as he put it. Carlos never again took a job, and he openly taunted his father by saying that he would live off the old man until he died. He also mocked his stepfather's ninth-grade education. He did this even though he was in the tenth grade himself for the third time, and there was no possibility that he could graduate from high school before the state kicked him out at the age of twenty-one.

Perhaps the worst thing about Carlos Romero, Jr., were his runins with the law. He had been picked up at least once a year since the age of twelve. Since he obtained his car at the age of eighteen (no one ever asked how), he had spent at least one night a month in a jail cell. He had perpetrated his most heinous crime about six months prior to this story when he sold his stepfather's house and farm to a young man from another town. Since proving the forgery would have been costly and time-consuming, Carlos senior opted to simply buy back his own farm for only a little over the three thousand dollars that the young man had paid for it. More recently, junior had wrecked his car by plowing it into a cow that had wandered onto the road. This he did while sober and in broad daylight. Apparently he was simply out to kill the cow.

But no matter what little troubles Carlos Romero, Jr., got himself into or what grief he caused other people, he was no rapist. He was just a tall, gangly young rogue with shoulder-length, wavy, black hair and the beginnings of a goatee—fuzz really. His only truly outstanding trait was stupidity, and when he played with the preteen boys in the neighborhood, he seemed to blend right in mentally. Still, even though Collazo didn't really think the young man had committed the attack on Luisa Ferré, he did think Carlos might know something, maybe saw something.

"Are you Carlos Romero, Jr?" Collazo asked.

He knew nothing about the young man's history, so he was not yet inclined to think ill of him, but he noticed a slight squint when he addressed the boy and didn't like it.

"Who are you?" Carlos replied.

"I'm Sheriff's Deputy Collazo from Angustias. Are you Carlos Romero, Jr?"

Collazo insisted on getting the young man's name because he had in mind that police work should be done in an orderly fashion, and this seemed like the natural place to begin his questioning. Otherwise his ideas about police work had been formed while a young man who walked miles to see a movie once a month. But this was long before Miranda rights and many other interventions by the Supreme Court, and he could never be convinced that the Supreme Court justices had intervened rationally and for the good of the population at large.

"What do you want to know my name for?"

"What do you want to hide your name for?" Collazo responded angrily.

He was hardly prepared to fight a war of wits with a smart aleck at that hour. Without realizing it, he put his hand on his night stick.

Carlos saw this move and responded by thrusting his wrists together in Collazo's face.

"Arrest me now because I'm not saying anything until I get a lawyer."

Collazo calmly did as suggested.

"Hey! What are you doing?" junior asked. He, at least, had been bluffing.

Collazo did not respond. He would let Gonzalo do the questioning. He put the young man in the back seat of the car and drove off.

The stepfather watched the arrest without saying a word. Carlos, Jr., was shouting something from the back seat of the car, but the windows were rolled up; it was impossible to hear anything clearly. When Collazo pulled away, Carlos, Sr., smiled to himself and decided he would spend the rest of the day in his twice-purchased fields, humming and far from the house phone.

Collazo brought the young man back to the Angustias station house but had no more cell space for him. Ferré was sound asleep by this time and could not have been awakened even with a hot branding iron. Collazo paused a moment, going over his options.

"Hey, mister. My arms are beginning to hurt," said Carlos.

He twisted himself so that his cuffed wrists were on his left side. He waggled them for Collazo's benefit.

"I said my arms hurt. My shoulders, they hurt."

It would have been clear to most that Carlos wanted to be released from the handcuffs, but this construal of Carlos's complaint never occurred to Collazo. He did realize that Gonzalo would want something done to alleviate the young man's discomfort, so he made a mental note to himself to remember to bring an ointment from home. Until then he would use a second pair of cuffs to leave Carlos chained to the bars of the cell.

"Hey!" Carlos yelled as Collazo was about to leave the room. "Are you just going to leave me standing here?"

Collazo brought a chair close to the prisoner, and then walked away. There were no weapons kept near Carlos, and Collazo took all the keys with him as he left. If Carlos got out of his handcuffs, he might vandalize the precinct, but he wouldn't be setting Francisco Ferré free.

When Collazo had left the building, Carlos used his feet to shift the chair into position behind himself, and then he found that he was chained just high enough on the cell bars to break his shoulders if he tried to sit.

"*Que cojones*. Did you see that guy?" he asked Ferré.

Ferré mumbled something in his sleep and settled himself.

"Lucky bastard," Carlos said, envying Ferré's mattress.

Collazo drove to the clinic. He reported the arrest of Carlos Romero and got instructions from Gonzalo.

"Go to Ferré's house. Find the mayor; he can get you a warrant for Ferré's house and property. Look for her clothes. Anything torn, bloody. Look for any blunt instruments that might have been used on her. Look for signs of a struggle. Get my camera from home. Keep a record."

"What do I tell Yolanda?"

This was a serious question, but Gonzalo had already thought out what Yolanda should be told.

"Tell her the truth. To a point. Tell her Francisco is being held on a drunk and disorderly charge, but that we're looking into more serious charges which we can't go into with her. In fact, see if you can get some information from her. Can she vouch for him? Does she know where he was after you dropped him off? Things like that. While you're at it, see if she's bruised."

"What if she's dead?" Collazo asked. He was fond of watching lurid crime shows on television and of reading cheap detective magazines and novels. Gonzalo, who was not fond of these things at all, was taken aback by the question.

"Dead? Come on. Just get over there. If I'm lucky, the doctor's going to wake Luisa up in a few minutes." He was on the verge of turning away from Collazo; then he added as an afterthought, "When you're done with Ferré's property, check the roads between Ferré's house and Mendoza's field. The clothes have to be somewhere."

Collazo left and Gonzalo went over to the doctor's office and knocked.

Doctor Perez looked tired when he opened the door.

"What?" he asked.

"I really need to speak with Luisa," Gonzalo said.

"I thought I made clear that I wasn't going to wake her just so you can have a chat."

Gonzalo nodded. He understood the doctor's position. If he were a doctor, he'd have said the same thing. God hadn't seen fit to order things that way.

"I don't think that's going to be good enough," he said.

Doctor Perez opened and closed his mouth, wasn't sure what to say.

"I make the medical decisions here," is what he decided on.

"I'm about to charge her father with the attack," Gonzalo said. "I would like to hear from her before I do that."

Doctor Perez sighed and rolled his eyes. He would have liked to say it wasn't his problem, but even though he hadn't been born in Angustias, he knew that if Francisco Ferré were charged with this crime, his life as he had known it would be over.

"All right," he said. "Give me two minutes. And let me tell you something, sheriff; she'll be awake but it'll be like talking to a drunk. A sleepy drunk."

With this, Gonzalo went into Luisa's room to wait for the doctor to wake her. While he waited, he reviewed his performance of the last few hours as sheriff. He didn't like what he brought to mind. So far, the night had been about being lost when it came to actual clues, barking out orders to his deputy, or meeting with the mayor. Under normal circumstances, Gonzalo took such a relaxed approach to his work, and to life in general, that only those who had gotten to know him over a long period of time, years, would believe that he could carry out the responsibilities of his position.

He was intelligent and proud of his intelligence. This pride was a reason why he wanted to have this case solved before the sheriff of Comerio started his shift at eight o'clock, and he was forced to ask for assistance. But pride wasn't the only reason. Gonzalo was a sensitive man in his way. Gonzalo was one of those people who truly could not see pain in others without feeling it themselves. He could not witness innocent suffering without wanting to alleviate it. He could not abide an abuse. The attack on Luisa, brutal as it must have been, galled him. He remembered her screams of just a few hours before, and he felt each scream as a stab. But he could do nothing to alleviate the pain that Luisa had endured; he could only avenge it. It was on this task that he concentrated his energies.

It was a little after six in the morning when the doctor walked into the room. He had changed clothes and had on bell-bottom, polyester slacks, though even Gonzalo was sure they had already passed out of fashion. He smiled at Gonzalo as he entered the room. He took hold of Luisa's wrist to take her pulse; a quarter of a minute later, he brought out a plastic-wrapped syringe and small bottle from the hip pocket of his smock. He found a spot on her thigh, and she began to stir. He peered into her eyes with a small flashlight while she held a thermometer in her mouth. When he had checked her temperature, he listened to her chest and gently felt her ribs. Then he walked over to Gonzalo and reported that she was in fair condition and could answer a few questions. Gonzalo thought for a moment about getting his wife to ask the questions, but he let her wait outside. He would have loved nothing better than to have a woman question the girl.

Luisa was stretching her arms out into the air above her and smiled at Gonzalo as he approached her. Gonzalo knew that, for the moment, Luisa had forgotten about the attack. He smiled at her as she flexed her feet and pointed her toes. It took only a few seconds for her smile to disappear as she realized where she was and why Gonzalo was there. Gonzalo, too, lost his smile.

"How are you feeling, Luisa?" he asked. "The doctor says you're going to do okay."

There was a strained pause, but she didn't say anything.

"I need to ask you a few questions about last night. It shouldn't take more than ten minutes," he said. She looked away from him, and he waited a minute, giving her time to compose herself.

"I don't remember too much about last night," she said.

"Tell me what you remember. What did you do after I sent you home last night? What happened when I left Mendoza's field?"

"Nothing," Luisa said. Tears began to form in her eyes, and Gonzalo knew he had only a few minutes more before she became too excited to question.

"Did you go straight home? Did you go to another field?" he asked. "Did you go to Comerio?" In one set of questions, he implicated both the men he had in custody. He wanted to see if she reacted more strongly to one question than to the others, but she had strong reactions to all three. She began to weep openly.

"Did you go home?" he asked again.

"Yes."

"Did Carlos take you home?"

"Yes."

"Did he attack you in any way?" At this question, Luisa began to sob loudly. Mari showed herself at the doorway.

"Luisa. Please understand. I need to know this. Did Carlos attack you at all?"

"No," she said.

"Would you like to name your attacker?"

Luisa turned completely away from Gonzalo, sobbing so loudly that the doctor and nurse both came into the room.

"I can't," she said, using the cast on her arm to wipe her nose. "I can't," she yelled. "Don't you see? I can't."

The doctor stepped between Gonzalo and Luisa and gave her an injection. He glared at Gonzalo.

"That's enough," he said.

While the truth of this case will come out soon enough, it is important that some light be shed on Luisa's part in this conversation.

Luisa was a good girl, much like Gonzalo's own daughters. She had not begun to misbehave until the semester before when she entered the tenth grade and met Carlos Romero. It was then that she began to occasionally keep late hours, drank her first beer, and became sexually active. Even with this change in her behavior, she never acted out of malice. When she lied to Gonzalo during this brief interview, it was out of a mixture of confusion and fear and disgrace, not from any evil intention. In Luisa's defense, she did tell some truths during the interview, and Gonzalo had not done the best job in questioning her.

In Gonzalo's years of interrogations, he had had reason to question only a dozen or so women. In all the cases except one, the issue was domestic: Either the husbands had beaten the women or the women had beaten their husbands. Whether they were victims or perpetrators, the women had always been seething with anger and more than willing to speak out their minds. Taking their statements had hardly required questioning at all. The only case that did not involve domestic violence was of a palm reader whose clientele was all male. When Gonzalo questioned her, she quickly admitted her prostitution, and when she was sent to San Juan to stand trial, she escaped. It was with this lack of experience that Gonzalo had approached Luisa's bedside. His only thought was to get information from her before she broke down crying. He also was confused, unsure of what questions to ask. More importantly, with Luisa getting so emotional so fast, Gonzalo couldn't bring himself to ask the pivotal question, "Did your father do this?" In this way he botched the interrogation.

When asked what had happened after he sent them home, she answered him truthfully: "Nothing." But Gonzalo had in mind the two o'clock visit to the field, while Luisa knew only of the midnight visit. Luisa and Carlos Romero had left the field walking about ten minutes before Gonzalo's second trip to Mendoza's pasture. When asked if she had gone home, if Carlos had accompanied her home, she had lied. Carlos and she had not gone to her house. They had gone to a more secluded place where neither the sheriff nor his deputy would interrupt. In any event, she had lied out of shame. She had chosen not to go home, and, for her misdeed, she had suffered terrible consequences. She told Gonzalo she had gone home because she wanted to cover over the fact that she had acted imprudently. She had no idea that this lie would implicate her father. In fact, had she known that her father was in jail, she would have told the truth. For all his faults, she loved him with a sincerity that is usually found only in the young.

As to whether Carlos had attacked her, Luisa had technically told the truth. Carlos had not actually attacked her, though what he did do was perhaps worse. Finally, when Luisa said she could not name her attacker, she was telling the truth. Not that she had no names to give Gonzalo. But the names she had were tied to her in disgrace, and she certainly was not ready to mention them willingly.

She might have told him of Carlos's role in the matter, but she was ashamed of her own behavior, which she saw as nearly as bad as her boyfriend's. She was afraid of what her parents might think of her if the whole truth came out. She was, after all, still only a teenager. Also, she was not yet quite sure that Carlos had done anything unlawful against her, though she certainly felt ill-used by him. It had not occurred to her that the semen found in her would have caused anyone to suspect more than the tryst she had consented to after Gonzalo had sent her home.

CHAPTER NINE

Luisa's mother, Yolanda Ferré, was still a young woman at the time of the attack. She had passed forty years of age more than a half-dozen years earlier, but her looks had not yet begun to betray her. She was still tall and unstooped; her skin was still tan, fresh, and bright, and wrinkles had only just begun to assert themselves about her eyes and mouth. Her hair was waist long and black with only a little gray; hardly mentionable gray. Her eyes were a lustrous light brown, and her smile revealed a perfect set of teeth; and though she'd been married for years, it still inspired men to think of themselves that they might yet be better than what they were.

These, of course, were the attributes that first caught hold of Francisco Ferré's imagination, but Yolanda had already earned a reputation for sainthood when he first noticed her in the months before leaving for Korea, and this too attracted him.

Like many of the young ladies of Angustias growing up in the

1940's, Yolanda was raised in a strictly religious, Roman Catholic family. There was, in fact, no other type of family in Angustias at the time. Like others before her, she was a star of Bethlehem as a child in the church Christmas drama. Like others, she became a Daughter of Mary as a preteen. And like others, she attended early Sunday Mass faithfully. Unlike most of the others, however, Yolanda did all this and much more with a true, understanding devotion. The worst of the young ladies of her time could put on and take off their religion like a shawl. Most of the young ladies believed what they had been told and behaved in the ways requested of them, but their religion, their beliefs were not really theirs. With Yolanda it was clear that her religion was her own. After much thought and grave consideration (more thought and graver consideration than even Padre Perea, her priest, gave), Yolanda believed her beliefs still. But her devotion was merely one sign of her spiritual life.

At about the age of ten, Yolanda served as God's instrument in performing a miracle. It was worse than useless to ask what the miracle was; no one remembers anymore with any accuracy, and Yolanda doesn't talk about it with anyone. Even the wildest rumors don't make the miracle out to be anything grand: None of the dead were raised from their graves; she didn't levitate off the ground. Some say that she was asked to pray for someone who was sick, and the person recovered. Not so very spectacular. Other young ladies in Puerto Rico have claimed to have been used by God (in fact, in Angustias alone there have been reports of several supposed immaculate conceptions), but Yolanda is the only person who is wholeheartedly believed. She is believed, in part, because she has never made the claim for herself.

Her reserve, her devotion to God, the miracle—all these things added up in the minds of her fellow townsfolk. By her mid-teens, the elders of Angustias would come to her with problems, seeking direction, like visiting an oracle. They never left her without feeling that the solution had been presented to them. One of those solutions came when Yolanda was about twenty years old, after a hurricane had passed over the island, causing a mud slide in Angustias. The mud brought more than twenty homes off the hills and into the valley, destroying every crop in its path. "What should we do?" They asked her. "Wait," she answered. "God will cause the crops to come again in their time. Rebuild the homes of the destitute and wait." Now there is nothing special about this advice. In fact, it might be difficult to think of a different course of action. Still, the people of Angustias thought the message was from God himself. Yolanda has been asked about this particular bit of wisdom: "Was there anything special about the message?" Yolanda just smiled and said, "Not that I know of. It just sounded reasonable at the time." Her levelheadedness is one more of her attractive qualities.

Some of these qualities had been passed on to Luisa. Luisa is now nearing forty years of age herself. While her beauty is different from that of her mother (Luisa is delicate and small while her mother is tall and large framed), she has her mother's characteristic smile and eyes. In her girlhood, however, Luisa's hair was worn shorter than her mother's and curled where Yolanda's was straight. Her temperament is a trait inherited from her father. Sadly, that would include an inability to forgive herself.

Luisa Ferré had grown up intelligent. She had excellent grades in school until just a few months before the attack. Besides her grades, one could see her intelligence in her face. She often had the knit brow of a scholar, and she looked archly at anyone who told hard-to-believe tales. In contrast, her classmates never wore a knit brow except at test time, the only time when they wished they had studied, and they never looked archly at anyone. After all, who would tell a story that contained elements of untruth?

Luisa was also often stubborn like her father, and, like her father, she could occasionally suffer through a fit of blinding rage. As a child, she had gone through some terrific tantrums, banging her head on the floor and pulling out her own hair. She would scratch herself until she bled and scream out curses randomly. This behavior stopped, more or less, soon after she entered school. By the time of the attack, she had learned to direct her anger to its cause. In this way she had several times exchanged sharp words with a few of her classmates and with her parents. Still, she was well liked since she was of a genuinely generous spirit and she was always ready with a joke. She never failed to make others laugh except in those rare times when she herself found nothing funny.

Her teachers asked themselves why she was showing the rebellious attitude this particular year. Part of this we could mark down to the obvious. She was developing into a woman, and, along with the pleasing encouragements of the teenage boys around her, she wanted the freedom to explore this womanhood more fully. She thought it was time for her to take charge of her own life. When she looked to her parents, she found them restricting. (What parents in Angustias weren't equally restrictive if not more so? Few parents were less demanding.) And she found them small. Like her parents, she was of a quick mind, but she had had opportunities to learn that were denied to them. How troubling it is to the teenage mind to be able to defeat parents in argument but still have to remain under their control. But this was only one of the reasons behind her rebelliousness.

Though Luisa was an intelligent girl, she was still a girl. When she fell in love, having never done that before, she did it badly. Carlos Romero was the first of the young men in her school to pay attention to her. He spoke to her and made her blush. He gave her flowers picked from the roadside and recited poems and whispered flatteries that had worked before. She did not realize in her infatuation that he paid equal attention to most of the pretty girls in hill towns of southern Puerto Rico. In fact, he didn't even have to explain away the attention he paid to other girls right in front of Luisa; Luisa herself did this for him.

After attending several car parties on Friday nights, Carlos began to lay siege to her chastity. He waited until another couple started toward the tall grass; then he asked if she would like to follow them. She paused and thought a moment, and, just as he was about to explain that they didn't have to do anything more than neck, she said yes. She cried during the act, but Carlos didn't notice. When it was over, she clung to him, both naked in the grass, and fell asleep. This was a nuisance to Carlos as he wanted to get his clothes back on before the insects found him, but it was a nuisance he had to endure, bored and staring up into the night sky.

That she might have become pregnant from this trip into the grass did not occur to her until Carlos was driving her home later that night. Then she turned to him and smiled and touched his face softly. Carlos did not notice this either, but she was thinking of the child they might have conceived and the happy family they would all make. She went to the clinic the next day for birth control. At the time, she was only thinking that she did not want to ruin Carlos's chances in life by becoming a burden to him. She did not then understand that Carlos would never have allowed her to be a burden to him, and, in any event, he was not the type of person destined even for mediocrity; he had no chances that she could have ruined.

The effect his wife and daughter had on Francisco Ferré was enormous. Though he was physically very strong and of a somewhat above-average intellect, he was also weak morally. After coming back from the war, he suffered from frequent periods of indecision. The whole town knew of this, and they knew that if he were left to make important choices on his own, he would make the wrong one every time. *"El Diablo me empuja,"* he would say. "The Devil pushes me." Most of the local population interpreted this to mean that his poor judgment was due to a local sugarcane rum popularly called *El Meao del Diablo,* The Devil's Piss. This rum was mixed with spices, and it was so strong that it could make a drinking man's eyes water just by sniffing its aroma. Francisco, of course, meant that the Devil had more control over him than he did. Only the women in his life could have more control than the Devil did.

Francisco doted on his two girls, as he called them. In the odd week when he did hire himself out to work on someone's land, it was because he was desperate to buy something for his wife. The last time he had worked his own farm had been for Luisa's benefit. Yolanda had told him that they had to begin some sort of college fund for her, and that year he brought in a harvest worth some eight thousand dollars. He put that money in the bank where it would sit quietly collecting interest until Luisa put it to its intended use. Not even the Devil could push him to touch it. In fact, the townspeople all knew that if Yolanda were only a more demanding wife, if only she made even a few more demands, he would have worked himself to death to supply her wants. But, as she reminded people, she didn't want a dead husband.

Strangely, though he was ready to jump through hoops for his wife and daughter, though he was overprotective of them, he did not care as much for his twin sons. By the time of this story, the twins were full-grown men with their own children, but Francisco had never shown them the affection he showered liberally on his wife and daughter. This is not to say that he had abused them in any way, only that when Luisa was born and as she grew up, he could spend hours cuddling with her or being her strong pony or carrying her around the house as she dangled off his shoulders. He never had nearly as much time for his sons.

For many in town this was completely natural; after all, you didn't want your sons to grow up to be sissies. Many in Angustias held the theory, completely uncorroborated by fact, that Francisco had a different reason for being partial to Luisa. Conceived and born as she was after his midnight nightmare-induced attack on Yolanda, Luisa was a symbol of Yolanda's continuing love and acceptance of him. Since these feelings were precious to him beyond expression, he treated their representation, Luisa, with special care.

96

When Carlos Marrero made a lewd remark about her budding breasts some years earlier, the report of the jest reached Francisco's ears at home. He stormed out of the house, striding to Colmado Ruiz, his breath coming in hot snorts, his face red and contorted with rage. Yolanda ran alongside him, begging him to do nothing, to ignore the insult, but he could not hear anything but the joke. He entered the store where, as he suspected, Marrero had his belly to the bar. The men at the bar stopped drinking when Yolanda came in a step behind him yelling, *"Marrero, ¡defiéndate!"* "Defend yourself, Marrero!" But it was too late. Marrero's neck was already in the crook of Francisco's powerful left arm, and with his right hand Francisco was forcing the crook closed. Marrero's life was in a vise. *"¡Tiene navaja!"* someone yelled. "He has a knife!" Marrero had pulled a switchblade from his sock in the first seconds of his strangulation, but the vise had closed on him with such suddenness and force that it slipped from his fingers before he could use it. By the time it hit the ground, Marrero's face was turning dark red, almost black, his eyes were shutting though swollen, and he was drooling. Only the fact that Yolanda had grabbed Francisco's face between her palms, saying, *"¡No hagas esto!"* "Don't do this!" saved Marrero's life that night. Francisco relented, slamming Marrero to the floor so hard that the crack that was heard scared the store owner. He thought for a moment that his cement floor had been broken. In fact, the sound had come from Marrero's cheekbone. Marrero coughed and gasped convulsively, unconsciously, desperately, while Francisco glowered over him, feeling certain that Marrero had escaped the hand of justice unscathed in comparison to what should have happened to him.

Everyone in Angustias knew Francisco would have killed for his daughter. It was absurd for anyone to suspect him of harming a hair on her head. Nor would he have allowed anyone else to harm her if it were in his power to prevent it. When Collazo dropped him off at home the night before, he never thought that his daughter was anywhere but safe in bed. It is safe to say, that if he had held even the slightest suspicion of any trouble that night, he would have searched the countryside until he found his daughter and brought her home to safety. Francisco Ferré hurt his daughter? Impossible.

CHAPTER TEN

Don't talk to her about the incident."

Before leaving the clinic, Gonzalo warned the doctor and nurse against contaminating Luisa.

"Keep her away from other patients and staff. Don't even let her listen to the radio. I don't want her to start filling in gaps in her memory from the information you can give her, you understand me?"

"Don't worry, Gonzalo. After the way you left her, she's not going to talk to anyone else," the doctor warned.

He, too, was upset over the attack, and he was sure that Gonzalo wasn't going to catch any culprits by disturbing the patient under his care.

Gonzalo's next step was to check up on Collazo and interrogate the two men he had in custody. He was certain that one of them had committed the crime. This relieved some of the pressure on him. Though he would never have admitted it openly, at the moment that he left the clinic, his biggest worry was whether he would be able to wrap up the loose ends and charge the right suspect before the sheriff of Comerio went in to work at nine. Nine o'clock was also the time when he expected Yolanda Ferré to try to bail out her husband. He hoped to have clear and certain evidence long before Yolanda came to him.

"¿*Qué dices?*" he asked when he saw Collazo searching through the overgrowth on the Ferré property.

"Have you found anything?"

"No."

"No sign of struggle?"

"No."

"None of her clothing?"

"No," Collazo answered, looking up in annoyance.

"Did you check on the other side of the house?"

"Uh-huh."

"How about across the street?"

"It's all clear there."

"You checked the whole block?"

"Can't you see? It's all clear. The grass has been cut recently. You can't hide anything there."

Gonzalo paused a moment. He realized that this type of investigation was a strain on his deputy. Normally, Collazo would have awakened from a nap at about five. Instead he had been running around town since he came on duty six-and-a-half hours earlier. Still, he would have liked a civil tone from his deputy. He decided to avoid confrontation and change the subject.

"Have you seen Ramirez?"

"No. Probably went home."

"I'm going to take a look at Mendoza's field and the side of the road between here and there. Then I'm going to the station to start questioning them. I want you to come after me and search all that area more closely. The stuff has to be somewhere."

"Right. Anyway, I'm done with his property. Unless he dragged her a few hundred yards in without making a sound, nothing happened here."

"Take a closer look, Collazo; she might have walked with him for a while before he grabbed her."

Collazo gave a skeptical look.

"You never know."

Gonzalo made a brief search of the roadside between the Ferré home and Mendoza's fields. He found nothing but the usual litter. What he wanted was torn clothing or a matted area, signs of struggle or spots of blood. He found none of these. He found no signs that anything had happened at all.

It was nearing seven in the morning. Gonzalo sat frustrated in his car. He had been on the case since three in the morning and had no hard evidence; his interview with Luisa had been fruitless. If he had the nine-man force that Comerio had, he could have combed the fields a lot more closely by now. With that much manpower, he could have gathered enough evidence to close the case an hour ago.

"What are you looking for?" asked an old local farmer, ducking his head into the car window.

Gonzalo turned and stared in some surprise.

"Nothing." He turned the ignition key and put the car in gear.

"Did something happen last night?" the old man asked as Gonzalo sped away. All Gonzalo could think was, "Didn't that guy hear the screaming last night?"

He parked in front of the station again and waited a few minutes for seven o'clock to arrive. Across the street from him was a grocery store that also served coffee and buttered bread to the townspeople. Three elderly men stood in the doorway, sipping coffee and watching him. Gonzalo knew that if he stayed in the car for much longer, they would come over to him, asking questions.

When he walked into the station house, he found Carlos Romero kneeling on the chair, leaning against the cell bars, sleeping. Francisco Ferré was also sound asleep, his arm hanging off the side of the cot.

Gonzalo unchained Carlos from the bars and took him, still in handcuffs, to the lobby in the front area of the station. This was as far from Francisco as he could get. He ordered the youth to sit on an ancient sofa, but Carlos remained standing.

"Sit. I need to ask some questions. It's going to take a while."

Carlos still didn't sit. There was a sleepy defiance forming on his face. In sixteen years of policing, how many young men just like Carlos had stood in this same precinct thinking they were going to walk out free men and laugh at the sheriff later? For a moment, Gonzalo felt contempt for the prisoner. He had to remind himself that Carlos hadn't been charged with anything and wouldn't even be in the station house at all except that he'd asked Collazo to arrest him and Collazo tended to take people literally.

Gonzalo tried to size him up.

Carlos Romero was tall, with a medium frame but with very little on that frame. Still, he could have been called wiry rather than skinny, and he was certainly muscular enough to warrant suspicion in this attack. He wore his dark hair sloppily parted down the middle, and he had on a pair of dungarees and a tee shirt, both of them dirty enough to make you think he might have at some time in the past put in an honest day's work. His only striking feature were his eyes, which were a light blue. But even these eyes could not redeem his face with its pug nose, thick lips, and drawn cheeks. Gonzalo did not doubt that with all its faults, Romero's face had always had one constant admirer, Romero himself.

Of his character, Gonzalo, with little direct evidence to go on, took a guess—besides his (astonishing) ability to attract the fancy of one young woman, he couldn't imagine a redeeming quality for the young man in front of him.

Gonzalo checked himself. Almost said out loud, "I've got no proof of that." He was thinking that Carlos might be worthless in every way. He shook his head slightly to get back control of his thoughts and clear his mind.

"Undo the cuffs," Carlos demanded.

The marks of the bars were clear on his face, and he was in the mood to be humored; he was in the mood to make things difficult for his interrogator.

"You're a prisoner. Any time you are out of a cell, you will be in handcuffs. That's the policy. If you still want to stand, that's up to you. Now. Is your name Carlos Romero?"

"I'm not answering anything until I have a lawyer. I've been arrested before. I know my rights."

Gonzalo paused a moment. This was the height of frustration, to have a man with a record demand his rights.

"Fine. Let me chain you back to the cell." Gonzalo chained him back to the bars but lower down so that he could sit.

"You want a lawyer. Let me go get you one."

"Oh, and get me breakfast, too. In Comerio, they give you bacon and eggs with toast and coffee."

"Breakfast is at nine. No bacon. Do you want your phone call now, too?"

"Yeah. Let me call my girlfriend. She'll get me out of this."

If Gonzalo had known more about his prisoner, he would have known that this was not necessarily a reference to the victim lying on the clinic bed. For Carlos Romero the word girlfriend could stand for any of a half-dozen young girls. But Gonzalo misunderstood this remark to mean Luisa exclusively. Palming his forehead, he smashed Carlos's head into the bars behind him. He wanted to say, "If you talk about that girl again, I'll cut off your manhood." Instead, all he could do was growl into his ear, "Don't play with me." Carlos was so terrified by the look on the sheriff's face that he couldn't even whisper the, "Okay, okay" he wanted to say.

As soon as Gonzalo left the station house, Carlos started planning what he would say, though it was difficult since he didn't know what the sheriff wanted to hear. Still, a general strategy formed in his mind.

Carlos Romero was a liar. He had found early on that lying was a skill useful both for getting what he wanted and for avoiding what he disliked. Carlos lied constantly, and he lied well. He had studied the tones and gestures of successful liars, and he was an expert. The raised eyebrows and tilted head of slight surprise. The hand motions of "It's not my fault" and "I have nothing to do with that," the inflections that said "I've been misunderstood," and the furrowed brow of dismay—all of these he practiced daily and could perform at will. Neither Maria Garcia, who would be his lawyer, nor Gonzalo knew this when they asked their questions.

Carlos's reasons for lying were as varied as the hates and wants of his heart; for every season there was a lie. But during this investigation he lied mainly because he suspected his questioners' motives. As a man completely unworthy of trust, he could not imagine trustworthiness in others. This simple but real explanation was a reason for death to come to Angustias that day.

The sheriff walked as fast as he could without breaking into a jog. Technically there were three lawyers in Angustias, but in practice there was only one, and Gonzalo didn't particularly like her. She had just graduated a year or two before from some New York City law school. She said she was from Puerto Rico originally, but her Spanish was spoken like a Nuyorican. Nuyoricans, Puerto Ricans from New York, were outsiders, not to be trusted.

Maria Garcia lived in one of the better houses on the plaza. In the short time she had been in town, she had garnered all of the contract work in Angustias, and she was steadily taking on the work from the adjoining towns. Lawyers who had been in practice in Comerio and Aibonito for decades were losing out to her competition. They grumbled that it was because of her youth, her pretty face, and her shapely legs. To them it stood to reason that their male clients would go to her for their deeds and leases; she had charms that the clients could not resist and the lawyers could not match. And, of course, female clients would simply patronize one of their own; they simply felt more comfortable talking to another woman. In fact, even Gonzalo, who thought she was a bit haughty, knew that she was simply a better lawyer. The others had become complacent while she regularly worked six or seven days a week and ten or twelve hours a day. While other lawyers waited for chance encounters on the plaza or in a bar to inform their clients of how work was going on contracts, Maria phoned or drove out to see her clients even if it was just to say, "We'll have to wait a few more days." She worked hard and earned more and now owned one of the nicest homes in town.

But as Gonzalo crossed the plaza, he thought of one thing only: in what ways Maria Garcia could obstruct the interrogation.

"Sheriff." She was somewhat surprised to see him as she opened the door. "What can I do for you?"

Maria came to the door in a terry-cloth bathrobe with her hair in disarray. For some reason, Gonzalo found this attractive, but he got to the point.

"Can you serve as the attorney for a suspect I have in custody? Just through the initial interrogation."

"Uhhh . . . why don't you come in?"

Maria Garcia had never handled a criminal case of any sort, and she told Gonzalo this as soon as he entered, but she had always wanted to handle such a case. The thought of an impassioned plea to the jury or the Perry Mason cross-examination was exciting to her. Still, she knew there was no money in that field for women.

"Why don't you tell me something about the case, and I'll tell you if I think I can do it."

"Okay. I have a young man from Comerio in custody. I'm holding him for suspicion of physical and sexual assault. Luisa Ferré, a girl from the valley, was attacked last night sometime between about two and three in the morning. I saw her with the suspect at a car party last night, and it is commonly known that he is her boyfriend. Luisa is sedated right now and has not been able to speak about the attack yet." He threw in the last sentence to deflect curiosity from one obvious line of inquiry.

Maria thought a while in silence. This was just the type of case she had always wanted to argue, though she would have preferred to have been on the prosecution side of the rape case. She was going to take the case, and in her mind she began to prepare for the appeal. The grounds would be her inexperience. She would sacrifice her career for her client, arguing that it was her incompetence that caused the conviction.

All this thinking caused an uncomfortable silence that Gonzalo broke by asking, "So, will you do it?"

"Oh, yes, yes. Let me get dressed." She scurried into her bedroom.

She put on her glasses first. In her mind, they turned her into a woman to be reckoned with. She ran back into the living room while only in a slip and still buttoning her blouse.

"I forgot my orange juice," she said, taking a glass of juice back into her bedroom.

Gonzalo could only shake his head and think, "Nuyorican."

A few minutes later she was fully dressed and asked where the interrogation was to take place.

"In the station."

"There are no other prisoners or deputies or anyone else present, right?" she asked as they were headed for the door.

"Well, yes. I have another prisoner there, but he's asleep."

"Good," she said as they entered the sunlight. "That might be grounds for a dismissal of evidence collected during the deposition if another prisoner were listening in. It might seem like coercion. I certainly appreciate you making this job easier for me." She smiled. The thought entered Gonzalo's mind that rattlesnakes sometimes appear to smile too.

Gonzalo stopped.

"Okay. Where would you like to do this?"

"Anyplace where no one else can hear."

"How about your house?"

She instantly agreed and instantly regretted it. On the one hand, the battle would be fought on friendly territory; she thought this was of some tactical advantage. On the other hand, if this guy really was a rapist, she would be inviting him into her home. Once he went free on appeal (this was what she felt would happen) he might look her up.

They walked into the station house. Carlos was amazed at the sight of Maria.

"That's it?" he said.

"You asked for a lawyer. She's the best one in town."

"No wonder this town is the way it is. They let the girls do the men's work."

"Look, Romero, you can either answer my questions with your lawyer present or we can wait until Monday, okay? On Monday we can go into San Juan and get you a dozen lawyers if you want."

"Okay, whatever. At least she's good to look at."

Comments like these made Maria Garcia lose her romantic interest in the case. She realized the man in front of her, her client, was being charged with a serious offense; and, judging from his behavior, he might actually be guilty. Certainly, mounting his defense was not going to be fun.

"Turn around, lady. Let me have a good look."

"Can you take the cuffs off my client?" she asked.

"Sorry. Standard procedure when dealing with a prisoner. Especially since we're going outside."

"Take off that jacket; I can't see your chest."

"Let's go," Maria said. She was ready to have the interview over with.

When Gonzalo unchained him from the bars and Carlos yelped, she pretended not to notice. She thanked Gonzalo in her heart for whatever little evil he had inflicted on her client.

"Would either of you want something to drink?" she asked when they had seated themselves on her sofa.

"No?" she asked, ignoring the request Carlos made for rum.

"Could you wait outside while I debrief my client?" she asked Gonzalo, and he got up and waited right outside her door, letting the prisoner know he should behave. Once alone, Maria turned to her client.

"First of all, let us get something straight: I am not a chick, broad, or piece of anything, okay. I am the lawyer who will get you out of a lot of trouble. Do you understand me?"

Carlos hung his head low.

"If you make another insulting remark, I will leave you to get another lawyer in San Juan next week. Are we clear?"

"*Yes.*" He tried to put a bold face on his response, but it came out weak despite his effort.

"You are accused of rape and assault. What do you know of these charges?"

"*Rape?*" he asked in surprise. "Nothing. They never said anything to me."

"Do you know Luisa Ferré?"

"She's my girlfriend."

"Are you intimate with her?"

"Intimate? I don't know. We have sex, though. We had sex last night. I didn't rape her."

"If I ask Luisa, will she tell me what you just said?"

"She should. She's a Christian girl. She's not supposed to lie about anything."

"Right. Do you know anything about a beating or assault on her made late last night?"

"I never hit that girl. I didn't do nothing to her. I never touched her," Carlos implored.

"Except for the sex, you mean, right?"

"Right."

"All right, just a few more questions. Around what time were you with Luisa yesterday and where?"

"I picked her up about ten or eleven Friday night, and we went to a car party in a field that belongs to some guy named Mendoza."

Maria handled Mendoza's properties for him and knew their location and extent.

"When did you and Luisa part last night?"

"I went home at about . . . two? Two-thirty?" he asked, as though Maria ought to know.

"And Luisa?"

"What about her?"

"Did you drive her home?"

"Nah. I think she walked," he said, beginning to squirm.

"You let her walk at two-thirty in the morning?"

"Well . . . , it was getting late for me to be driving around."

"But it was okay for Luisa to walk home alone at that hour?"

Carlos shrugged.

Maria knew that there was probably more to the story, but she hardly suspected how much more there really was.

"Okay. You've been in custody since this morning?"

"Early this morning."

"What time?"

"About five, I think."

"What have they asked you so far, and what have you answered?"

"They keep asking me my name, but I haven't told them anything yet."

"You haven't even identified yourself?"

"I took the fifth."

"On your name?" Garcia paused. She wasn't sure you had a right to withhold your name. "Anyway. Do you have any idea what these charges might be about?"

"I don't need to rape nobody. I got looks."

Her client's looks were questionable at best. She decided that she wasn't going to get any useful information from her client. He seemed to have been truly shocked by the charges. She called Gonzalo back into the house. The questions he asked might be more helpful than her client was.

"We may begin," she said. It was already approaching seven-thirty.

"Good. State your name."

Carlos turned to her apprehensively. She nodded to him, and he answered.

"Carlos, you are being held because we suspect you may have been involved in an attack on Luisa Ferré last night. Do you know anything about this attack?"

"My client's position is that he was with Luisa for some part of last night, but that he left her in good health. He did not attack her, nor did he participate in any attack upon her. He is innocent of any charges related to this incident."

Of course, Maria Garcia was overstating the case. She was young and inexperienced. She thought the best strategy was to go on the verbal offensive, making grand claims in strong language. In fact, she should have recalled that her client had not yet been charged with anything. She should have realized that her debriefing of Carlos was insufficient for her to claim that he had nothing to do with the attack. Carlos had not exactly said that, though it was what he implied. Gonzalo understood her strategy and decided to go on a different tack.

"There was sperm found in Luisa's vagina. Are you telling me you let Luisa have sex with another man?"

This question was designed to anger Carlos into a response, and it did. Before Maria could say anything, Carlos jumped up with his answer.

"It was me that did it. We had sex last night. We have sex every Friday. If anything, she attacks me every weekend."

Maria was, of course, surprised by this answer. She hadn't expected Carlos to offer incriminating information so readily. On the other hand, Gonzalo got the answer he expected. He had expected Carlos to lie on this issue, and it was clear to him that he had. Gonzalo thought of Luisa as being virginal, as virginal as his own daughters were. In his opinion, Carlos's confession was no more than macho bragging. Any intercourse had to have been forced, and as of that moment, Gonzalo was sure Carlos had nothing to do with it. The guilt of Francisco Ferré in this matter seemed all the more certain.

"So you had sex with her?"

"My client has nothing further to say at this time," Maria said. She reached out and put a hand on Carlos's knee to keep him from talking. It didn't work.

"Every weekend, man. She's hot for me!"

"Sheriff, please! I need to talk with my client. I need to talk to him before the questioning goes any further!"

Except for asking him to tell her the whole truth and delaying any more admissions, Maria, at the moment, didn't really have a game plan. It hadn't crossed her mind that a client of hers would be so stupid as to implicate himself at just about every turn, and she could tell by the lines of Gonzalo's face that he was just getting more angry with every word Carlos spoke.

The sheriff made a move toward Carlos.

"Counsel, I need to put your client away for a while. I need to question other people."

"I need to talk to him," Maria said firmly. "You can't prohibit me from speaking to my client!"

"Fine," Gonzalo said. He then produced the second pair of handcuffs and chained Carlos to a heavy, wooden coffee table.

"I'm going to deputize the mayor. He'll be here in about two minutes. After that, I'll be in the station house."

As soon as the sheriff was out of the house, Maria turned to her client and sighed.

"My God, you're stupid," she said.

He leered a smile at her.

"You want me?" he asked. He was serious.

Maria put a hand to her forehead to keep her head from exploding.

As Gonzalo walked to the mayor's house only a few doors away, he noticed that the three elderly men from the grocery store were watching him from the plaza now, and they had been joined by four or five other men and women. His policy would be to say nothing to them, no matter what they asked. He would make sure that Maria Garcia did not speak to them either. Collazo could be trusted to leak nothing of the crime or the investigation through a natural disinclination to talk. The mayor was naturally voluble, but Gonzalo would impress upon him the need for silence in this case, and he had no doubt of his compliance given the nature of the crime and the youth of the victim. Thinking all this, he knocked on the mayor's door.

CHAPTER ELEVEN

Mayor Ramirez's door was opened by his maid. He was the only man in Angustias to retain a servant of any type, and he did this though he could only barely afford one. He had grown up in Angustias during the thirties and forties, and, while others in town suffered through a long and profound Depression, his family had always been well off. The Ramirezes had always retained several house servants, but during the relative prosperity of the fifties and sixties, their fortunes had declined. The Mendozas, the richest family in Angustias for more than a century, had bought up most of the Ramirez property. The mayor was left with the house on the plaza and a small, hilly farm in the valley. This property had never been farmed until the mayor had put the plow to it in the seventies. Though he was more than forty years old by then, this was the first manual labor he had ever done, and he did his work surprisingly well. The farm paid for the domestic and the occasional new car.

Rafael Ramirez was a proud man. Since inheriting the remnant of his father's property, he had struggled to pay off debts and regain the prestige of his family name. Part of his plan had been to become mayor. This was his third term in office, and, while he didn't do a spectacular job as mayor, he also didn't do any worse than those who had come before him. During an election year, he walked about town with such a ferocious look in his eyes, shaking hands savagely and slapping the backs of even the very elderly so hard they nearly coughed up their souls, that he frightened contenders. Winning was so clearly important to him that the people were afraid of what might happen to him if he lost an election. He was already planning his fourth campaign, though he wasn't yet halfway through his third term.

"Gonzalo," said the maid in some surprise.

"Rosa. Is the mayor up?"

"Yes, yes. He's in his library." The mayor was a fond reader of biographies, and he considered the room where he kept his hundred or so books to be his library, though a large and costly pool table actually dominated the room.

Rosa led the way, but, before reaching the door, she turned.

"Have you caught him?" she asked.

"Who?"

"The rapist. The man who attacked Luisa. Who else?"

Gonzalo said nothing. If Rosa knew, the whole town would know soon. She stood on tippie-toes to whisper into his ear.

"I've known Francisco Ferré since he was a child. It could not have been him," she said.

"Not him." With this, she opened the door, and Gonzalo stepped in.

The first person Gonzalo recognized as he walked into the library was the mayor, but he quickly recognized all of the others. There was the sheriff of Comerio and his deputy, both in their street clothes; the mayor's assistant, Manuel Hernandez; Angustias's treasurer, Roberto Colon, and two or three other important townspeople. Gonzalo swallowed so hard he thought for a moment that he could literally feel his heart sink. Not only did his town know, but the town of Comerio knew, their sheriff knew. He would offer to help, to meddle, to take over.

"Come in, Gonzalo. I was just about to send someone to look for you." Gonzalo closed the door behind himself.

"How's the investigation going?" the mayor asked. "Have you gotten any information out of Ferré yet? Did you find the site of the incident? How's Luisa?"

"Could I talk to you in private for a minute?" was Gonzalo's response.

In the hallway, he turned on his mayor.

"Why do all those people know about this crime? This kind of investigation should be kept quiet. There is no need for this information to go out to the public. The man we want for the crime is in custody. This is improper. Completely improper."

The mayor was hardly the man to be cowed by having his improprieties pointed out to him. He, in turn, turned on his sheriff.

"Francisco is in jail, but how much proof have you collected in four hours?" he asked. "If his daughter refuses to testify against him, can you put him away? Do you have any of the clothes? I drove back into the valley to help with the search. Collazo started to look around without even knowing what to look for. You need more people out in the field if you want to wrap this up quickly. Are your feelings hurt? Are they?" he asked, growing red.

"Well, I don't give a damn," the mayor went on. "Francisco Ferré should hang for what he did, and I would do it myself if it were possible. Now you go in there and listen to what we have to say. Remember, all of us want to wrap this up today. We're all on the same team."

With that, the two men returned to the library.

"Now sheriff," the mayor began, talking to the sheriff of Comerio. "Tell us what you're doing."

Sheriff Molina of Comerio, a man about fifteen years older than Gonzalo, had been such a rabble-rouser in his youth that he was thought to have been a splinter off of Satan. Now he was much quieted down, but he was still thought to occasionally abuse prisoners who were handcuffed; he laughed whenever anyone brought this rumor up, and it is impossible to tell whether this claim had anything of truth in it.

"I have put ten men in the fields, five of my deputies and five of the most respected men of Comerio. They're looking through every farm from Colmado Ruiz to Mendoza's field. My other deputies are also busy. Since she goes to school in Comerio, I have them talking to her teachers to see if there is anyone else who might have done this thing besides her father."

"I think you're barking up the wrong tree there. We have the right man," Ramirez said.

"Well, it couldn't hurt to be sure. Now, sheriff," he said, addressing Gonzalo. "Is there anything else you need or want for this investigation?"

Gonzalo thought a moment.

"Do you know anything about a young man from your town named Carlos Romero?"

"Yeah, I know Carlos. Why? Is he a suspect?"

"Not really, but he was with her last night. He says he left her and doesn't know anything about what might have happened to her. I think he's telling the truth, but he might have more to say."

"You questioned him already?"

"Yes."

"And you think he's holding back?"

"Maybe."

"If you let me question him, I'll get everything from him. Me and Carlos go back a few years. I know how to treat him just right."

"Fine, but he has a lawyer."

The smile that was forming on Molina's face dissolved.

"That's okay. I don't need to touch him to get what I want."

"Good. He's in Maria Garcia's house. The mayor can show you the way. I'll meet you there later."

"Where are you going?" Ramirez asked.

"I've got a lot of people to talk to before Yolanda comes to bail him out." And with that, he left the room.

In the Ferré home, Yolanda was preparing for a walk into town, for a trip to the bank and to Gonzalo's office. There was no rush. Francisco was never very anxious to leave, especially not if he had gotten very drunk. In fact, she knew there was a good possibility that he was still sound asleep in the cell, and she would have to wait for him to sober a little before he could walk home. The walk, in fact, was part of the sobering process; town was about an hour's walk distant. She knew also that if Francisco had gotten into a fight, if he had hurt someone or broken some furniture in Colmado Ruiz, there would be fines and damages to pay, more paperwork to fill out, and, in fact, Gonzalo might decide to keep Francisco until Monday to teach him a lesson and appease the injured party. She knew all of this and so she was in no hurry.

It occurred to her as she swept up her hair into a waist-length ponytail, that her husband might have done some real harm to someone. She knew his strength and his rage and she feared that one day he would go too far and someone would be dead. In her mind, for a brief moment, she saw the picture of her husband's face contorted with intense fury and of his fingers wrapped around some poor offender's throat; the offender had no chance of course—the fingers would tighten their grasp until there was no air, and they would only release when there was no life. As this thought flashed through her mind, she brushed her own neck with her hand. She didn't think of the time when her own neck had been in the unforgiving clutch; she only felt an uneasiness that went unexplained.

She left her room and began breakfast. The eggs were from chickens that she tended, and the ham came from a hog Francisco had slaughtered; the coffee and the milk, likewise, came from their farm. The bread that she sliced and put into a toaster was from a *comadre* of hers that lived in the hills.

She moved through her kitchen in silence, giving Luisa a few extra minutes of sleep before she had to awaken her. She explained to neighbors a few days later, however, that there was that morning also a sense that she did not want to see her rebellious teen daughter any earlier than she needed to. Luisa had become a chore to deal with and there was no urgent desire to greet her that morning. Sooner or later, Luisa would say something disagreeable. While the food was cooking, it was better to stand and watch over it in the morning silence. Later, she would remember the few sounds of those minutes particularly well: outside, there were a few birds singing; a hummingbird stopped in midair to pick at a flower growing outside the kitchen window; at a great distance a hawk screeched. Inside, there was only the sound of the ham in its pan. Strange that she didn't remember the sound of the eggs frying in the pan.

As the coffee brewed and a minute or two before all the other elements of her breakfast were finished, she called out to Luisa. There was no response, but this was not unusual. Luisa had begun to avoid speaking to her parents whenever she could. It was as though they simply were not hip enough for her. She wanted to have her way in things without arguing the issue. Also, she had gotten into the habit of sleeping late on days when it was possible to do so; certainly a Saturday was such a day.

"Luisa, *ven a desayunar,*" her mother called out. "Luisa, come to breakfast." Still, there was no response. Yolanda walked over to the bedroom door.

"We have to go into town. Get dressed," she said, knocking lightly on the door.

When there was no response to her knocking, she opened the door and found the room empty. She went back to the kitchen, turned off the stove, and served herself an extra-large portion. It had already happened twice before that Luisa had decided late to stay in a friend's house without calling to say where she was. This lack of consideration had caused a great argument the first time, but Yolanda was determined to remain calm. Her husband needed her, and it did not occur to her that Luisa might not be safe. Certainly there was concern for the long term if Luisa continued to behave in this manner, but that concern would be expressed in a stern lecture later. For now, she thought only of the long walk to town and the forms she would have to fill out.

By the time Yolanda Ferré got out onto the street, it was a little past eight. She knew she would meet several of her neighbors on the road. There was no longer any embarrassment attached to bailing Francisco out for her. She knew that if she encountered enough people on the road, she would arrive in town well informed about the happenings of the night before. She would know if her husband had broken chairs or fought or if he had simply fallen asleep on the highway or cursed out some respectable widow. Years earlier, he had been arrested for pinching Lillian Rosario's buttocks while he was drunk; he had pinched hard enough to make her cry and to bruise her. Her husband saw the mark later that night, and Gonzalo was forced to arrest Francisco to keep Edward Rosario from getting to Francisco first.

She encountered her first informant after only ten minutes of walking. Doña Carmen, a reliable gossip for over fifty years, stopped her.

"*¡Ay, hija! ¿Es verdad?*" "Is it true, my daughter?" she asked. "Did he do it?" she asked, raising her wrinkled fingers to cover her wrinkled lips as though to hide from God the implications of what she asked.

"Do what?" Yolanda asked. The old woman's disturbed manner,

the fear in her eyes, caused Yolanda to worry. She knew her husband was capable of much—she had often feared that Francisco would drink to drunkenness once too often and do some terrible thing.

"Do what?" Yolanda insisted.

Doña Carmen opened her mouth to answer but stayed silent. There would be no easy way of saying this. An accusation of murder would have been an easy thing in comparison.

"Let me walk with you," Doña Carmen said, putting her arm in Yolanda's arm, and the two women started up the hill, out of the valley, and into town.

In town, Francisco Ferré was still asleep on his cot in his cell, but he was watched by a hundred eyes. The back wall of his cell was solid. This is where the station house was joined to the government building. The cot was arranged lengthwise along this wall. The wall to the left and right of the cot, however, had iron barred windows.

The station house was built in a time when liberals ran the town, and they thought it would be a humanitarian gesture to let the prisoners have a view of the outside world. It did not dawn on them that the outside world would also have a view of the prisoners, that victims might come by to exact revenge upon their caged attackers, that drunks might be given an endless supply of drink by their friends, that enraged inmates might curse and spit at innocent passersby. It did not occur to the developers of the cell that one day Francisco Ferré might lie on the cot, innocent of any crime, reaping the rancor of his neighbors. People who had known him since childhood, for fifty years, looked at him in his drunken sleep, looked at him in their growing hate, looked at him not knowing what to say or do but needing to say and do something.

In no one's memory had such a crime, the rape of a daughter by her father, gone without swift and severe punishment. In fact, only a dozen years earlier, a man accused by his wife of molesting their young daughter had been beaten savagely at Colmado Ruiz. He survived and was let go, but was later found in his own fields, having bled to death—after a castration with his own machete. Gonzalo pursued the case, but he knew it was hopeless; he was hired to enforce the law, and, in the end, laws are often the expression of the people's limited ability to tolerate certain behavior. While the town could not tolerate a child molester, they certainly could tolerate, applaud even, the vigilante who brought what they sensed was justice.

The reclining form of Francisco Ferré presented his audience with the view of a man who had committed the worst of crimes, the gravest of sins, but who was resting, having escaped punishment and justice. Worst of all, Ferré had deceived the town. He had been thought of as a neighbor and friend, he had been given credit in stores, he had been called upon for help in times of need, he had shaken hands with and said hello to everybody who now watched him, he had played with their children, but now it was clear, the mayor's friends had made it clear, that Francisco Ferré was not the man they had thought him to be. He was not a man at all. He was something far less than human, less than dog. He was something they had no name for, something that made them shiver in the heat of the rising sun.

As Gonzalo turned the corner, coming around the government building, he understood all that the people of his town felt. He knew how dangerous the people in the huddle about the window might be. He could not disperse them from the window or remove Francisco from the station house without facing a great deal of trouble. He headed straight for the door, but someone shouted after him.

"Are you going to bring him out? Are you going to get the *asesino*?"

Gonzalo stopped and smiled. He was now terrifically tired, and he sensed that his mind was slowing.

"Ferré didn't kill anyone."

"He raped his daughter!" someone shouted from behind him.

"Ferré is in jail for being drunk and disorderly," Gonzalo answered.

"The mayor's friends said he raped his daughter," said a lady.

Gonzalo wondered how to answer this. He thought that if he revealed the capture of another suspect, Carlos Romero, that it might relieve some pressure at the station house. There again, it would do nothing good for Maria Garcia.

"We don't know who raped her," he said, though he was certain of Francisco's guilt. "We have several suspects in custody and several that we're looking for."

With that, he hurried in. He knew that if he stayed to argue the point the next question would be, "Where are the other suspects?" Half the town would want to be deputized. He thought he had cleverly said just enough to confuse the crowd, to throw them off the scent. In fact, no one believed him. They clearly saw only one prisoner. Remarkably, either no one had seen the comings and goings of Carlos Romero or they had misinterpreted his release to Maria Garcia's house or they simply preferred to believe the worst of their neighbor.

Somewhere a bottle broke as Gonzalo was closing the door, and he wondered: "Dropped or thrown?" Instantly, he decided to ignore it, but he looked into the crowd as the door came to within an inch of shut. It closed on a crowd glaring angry defiance at him. "Thrown," he decided.

CHAPTER TWELVE

While Gonzalo spent a few minutes of relative quiet in his station house trying to gather his thoughts before waking Ferré and interrogating him, Collazo was finding nothing that looked like a crime scene.

Unlike Gonzalo, Collazo was never proud of his intelligence. Instead, he valued his dogged determination and hard work. He preferred to have direct orders to follow and to be allowed to follow them. In this way his partnership with Gonzalo was a blessing for both men. Gonzalo liked to give orders and have them followed. It could be argued that on this day Gonzalo and Collazo both simply had too much to do and too little information to do it with. There is no doubt that these circumstances were the cause of some of the problems of that day.

By the time Yolanda Ferré left her house headed for town, Collazo had driven deeper into the valley to Mendoza's fields where the car party had been the night before. He had searched a great deal of the Ferré property without finding a single suspicious mark. He had, in fact, begun the search with little hope of finding anything useful. While Martin Mendoza's fields were densely covered with tall grasses, making it easy to notice when someone had recently been through, Ferré's field was either completely bare (where he might want to have a small kitchen garden) or covered with tall trees with little undergrowth. True, if there were a severe struggle, tree branches might be broken off. Also, there was the possibility of finding the torn clothes. But such a severe fight seemed unlikely to him. The neighbors would have heard something. No. In Collazo's thinking, if there was a fight, it occurred farther in the valley, on Mendoza's property where there were very few families living and most of them lived far from the road.

In truth, Collazo thought there was little in the way of fighting. He saw the scenario quite clearly in his mind. Ferré got drunk after he was dropped off and went for a walk looking for the "lucky" woman he had talked of earlier. He found his own daughter somewhere deep in the valley, probably walking home from the car party. She, unaware of what was on her father's mind, greeted him without hesitation. He, with sinful lust in control, subdued her in seconds, belaboring her face and body with blows forceful enough to crumple a man. There were no screams, no time for screams. Then the monster was on her. Collazo could get no further than this. His mind went to blackness and rage thinking of Ferré forcing his own child to the ground. He was beginning to think of the futility of punishment in such a case. Why not let Ferré go? Being such a thing as he was, was that not punishment enough? Hell enough? If he did not suffer to know his guilt in such a matter, what punishment could do more? With these thoughts in mind, he searched Mendoza's field fruitlessly.

Where the car party had been, there were several areas of matted grass. These registered as sin in Collazo's mind, but as relatively harmless sin. He well knew that if he had not married early, he might have been guilty of the same. There were a multitude of cigarette butts where the cars had been. Some beer bottles as well. Vice was bad, he thought. He inspected each of the matted areas closely. Each area had a matted path leading to it. The first one he examined revealed some spilled pocket change. This he collected absentmindedly. He didn't think of it as evidence but didn't want to waste it. There was nothing suspicious at this area.

He followed a second matted path a few feet in. He heard the loud buzz of dozens of giant flies. He continued on until several flies pelted his head and body, and the smell of dead dog turned him back. There had been no matted area at the end of this path, so he assumed the same smell had repelled the lovers of the night before.

The third path ended with a matted area. Collazo made a close examination of the area, finding a condom wrapper. At this, Collazo was grieved. The wrapper proved sin compounded on sin compounded on sin. The fornication might be excused as a passionate sin. The condom wrapper was a sin of its own. Even worse, the wrapper showed that the first sin had been premeditated; it showed that the fornication occurred after a trip to a pharmacy for preparation. From the days when he was young to then, when he was already *old,* sin had multiplied. He sighed at this and moved on to finish his investigation of the site.

Across the road from Mendoza's field was a steep declivity. It would have been a terrible struggle for Ferré to drag or carry his daughter down this hill any appreciable distance. Collazo knew from experience that a single misstep would have one sliding down the hill until stopped by a tree, and that sort of stop didn't leave one capable of doing much more than moaning for help. Besides, in Collazo's mind, Ferré had done the deed on the roadside. He was drunk and would not have bothered to drag the girl anywhere.

He drove slowly out of the valley, up from Mendoza's field, checking both sides of the road. But before announcing what evidence he collected and how he found it, we should remember Yolanda Ferré and Doña Carmen in their walk to town?

After walking a short space in silence, Yolanda spoke.

"What did you want to tell me?" she asked.

Doña Carmen remained mute a moment, slowing her pace.

"*Es duro,*" she said. "It is hard.

"Your husband is a good man. I have known him many years. Since he was born. I still remember that day. His mother and I played as children. What happened to him in the war damaged him, but he is still good."

Doña Carmen said all of this slowly, trying to prepare Yolanda for a terrible shock. In fact, all she was doing was creating an even greater tension within Yolanda. She formed the opinion that her husband must have committed some great crime to cause so long a preamble in a woman who was usually so ready to share a rumor. She envisioned for a moment that Marrero was on a hospital bed, wrapped in bloody bandages, in a coma.

"Doña Carmen, I know all of this already. Do you know why my husband is in jail?"

In truth, the old woman had a good, though not perfect, idea of why Francisco was jailed. It was part of the mayor's mischief that he had called many of the townspeople to question them after locking Francisco away. He called all of Yolanda's nearest neighbors and asked if they knew anything about Francisco's actions of the night before. When they asked why he wanted to know, he explained to them that "the bastard" had raped his daughter, and a case was being put together. Doña Carmen had been one of the first to be called. Not only was she a close neighbor to the Ferré family, she was also well liked in town. Ramirez must have thought that the dissemination of the accusation against Ferré would have provoked a mob. He was angry with Ferré and would have liked a scene. He would have winked at a lynching.

Doña Carmen stopped. They stood on part of the road that was clear of overhanging branches. The morning sun was beginning to slice into their skin. The morning dew, which had cooled the air, had turned to mere humidity. There was a breeze that carried the scent of heavy rain in it. Doña Carmen, shriveled small and wrinkled, looked up into the eyes of Yolanda Ferré, and a tear escaped her eye.

"*Violó a Luisa,*" she said. "He violated Luisa."

Yolanda instantly raised her hand to strike Doña Carmen as a liar. Only her white hairs saved the old woman from the blow. But the woman begged to be hit.

"*Hit* me!" she screamed. "Hit me hard. I want to die for what I have just said. It kills me. But it is no less true because it is painful. *Hija mia.* What can I say? He is in jail because he raped his own daughter. He was drunk. He was crazy. The devil made him do it. I don't know what to say, Yoli. You are like a daughter to me. He is like a son. The girl is my baby. She lights up the world for me," the old woman said. "But the deed is done."

Yolanda's mind reeled in a nighttime darkness of grief. There were no words, no images, only pain. She swayed gently, and Doña Carmen reached out a hand to help steady her, but Yolanda batted it away. For a moment, her mind was a complete blank. From the pit of her stomach, she tried to verbalize something. She opened her mouth, but nothing, not even a groan or a yell, would come out. The old woman stood near her, wrenching her hands hard, not daring to comfort Yolanda in any way until she stooped to put her hands on her knees. From that position, she fell to the road, sitting, and Doña Carmen slowly knelt on the ground next to her and clasped Yolanda's head to her chest.

"Cry, my child. Cry. This is a tragedy for you. This is a tragedy for him as well. This is a tragedy for the world, and it is a tragedy for the girl."

Yolanda could not contain her tears, and for several minutes she wet the front of Doña Carmen's dress.

"Think of the girl, Yoli. Think of Luisa. She needs you now. She needs you to be strong for her. . . ."

"I'll kill him!" were the first words Yolanda said.

"No, *mi hija*. What would that do to help anything? That would only cause more trouble for everyone. Tell me, my child. If you did that, then who would survive from all this tragedy?"

At a great distance, a crack of thunder was heard. It was raining in Comerio, and Yolanda slowly picked herself up off the ground and continued her walk to town. Not a single clear thought developed in her mind in all the distance she traveled from that spot to the center of Angustias.

At about this time, Collazo was beginning his slow drive up out of the valley, searching both sides of the road for evidence. It was not too long before he came upon a farmer sitting by the roadside who waved at him to stop. Collazo pulled the car to the side of the road and the farmer stood up slowly, brushing the dirt off his trousers. Don José was only a little younger than Collazo, but he was much smaller and looked older by far. Collazo considered him an ignorant and dishonorable man. He was of the type who liked to egg on barroom brawlers but would rather curl up into a ball than fight if the option of running were cut off from him. Torturing rodents caught by glue traps is still his favorite pastime.

Don José ambled over to the car and ducked his head in the passenger-side window. His face and hair were greasy, and his beige work shirt was heavily stained with banana tree sap and sweat. Collazo guessed it hadn't been washed in months.

"*¿Que pasa, José?* I'm busy," Collazo called out from his car.

"Luisa was raped last night, right?"

Collazo rolled his eyes and shook his head. José lived so far out of town that if he knew, then there wasn't a person in Angustias who didn't know. He correctly suspected the mayor of revealing the information.

"*I* can't say anything about what you just said."

He was about to pull away, but José stopped him. He pulled a small, white sock from his pocket.

"Well, her clothes is all over my farm. Do you need to look at it, or can I put it in a bag and take it to her mother?"

Collazo was stunned for a moment. José's field was farther than Mendoza's. Deeper in the valley, it was the last property in Angustias before Comerio began. It was a few hundred yards farther down the road than where the car party had been. Assuming that Ferré did not drag her hundreds of yards, thousands of feet, what had she been doing so far from home, so close to Comerio?

"Should I give her the stuff? I have to get back to work; it's going to rain soon."

Collazo looked up at the horizon, and he could see the storm a few miles away.

"No. No. Her mother doesn't know anything yet. Get in."

José led Collazo to a path worn through the grass of his field and a clear area where there were several cigarette butts and beer cans. There were no condom wrappers here. Luisa's clothes were thrown about. Her pants and shirt were arranged on the ground neatly, as though used as a buffer against the cold damp grass during sex, but her bra and panties were high in trees. Her other sock was in tall grass some yards away, and her shoes thrown even farther. There were other signs of struggle. Thin broken branches on some of the nearby coffee trees and tiny drops of blood on grass leaves were evident on close inspection of the area. Whatever had happened the night before had certainly happened here, Collazo concluded. This was the first hard evidence collected (besides Luisa's condition) that anything criminal had happened. The site of the transgression had been ascertained, but now Collazo began to be doubtful about who had committed the offense.

"Touch nothing," he told José. "Talk to no one."

"Not even the mayor?" José asked.

"No one," was all Collazo responded.

With that, Collazo took the sock, got back into his car, and drove for town.

On his way out of the valley, he passed Yolanda Ferré, shocked and silent for some minutes now, and Doña Carmen. When Yolanda saw his car coming, she waved for him to stop and shouted to him, but he continued on, grimly shaking his head at her. He knew she was the last person he wanted to speak to, and he had what he thought of as urgent information for Gonzalo. As it turned out, he was stopped long before reaching town and Gonzalo, and Yolanda reached the station house before he did.

At the next curve, still some distance from Colmado Ruiz and the turn onto the road to town, the mayor flagged him down. Collazo would have loved to have kept on; Ramirez was second on his list of people to avoid. He felt a duty to stop, however.

"Where are you going so fast?" the mayor asked.

"I have evidence," was the reply.

"Really? Let me see."

Collazo was forced to take the mayor and some of the Comerio deputies to José's farm. Yolanda and Doña Carmen continued their walk into town, noticing the commotion and quickening their pace. Not another word was said between the two women.

After the mayor had seen all the details of the crime site, he ordered Collazo to accompany him to the clinic to interview Luisa. Collazo protested. The girl had already been questioned by Gonzalo.

"Did she tell him anything useful? I don't think he has the right touch for this kind of questioning. He's a good sheriff, but sometimes you need to handle people with delicacy."

"Are you more delicate than Gonzalo?" Collazo asked in some surprise. He thought perhaps the mayor had no sense of how offensive he often was.

"Not me, Collazo. But you are."

Collazo rolled his eyes and sighed again. Now that he considered the matter properly, there was no one else he wanted to speak to less than Luisa Ferré.

CHAPTER THIRTEEN

There was only one place Gonzalo could interrogate Francisco Ferré. He could not move him to another building, though he would have liked to interview him in the mayor's house. The crowds would not permit such a transfer. If someone had thrown a bottle at him, and he was sure that the bottle had been thrown, then there was no telling what might happen to the prisoner. He paused in thought a moment. Would he shoot into a mob to defend his prisoner? Silly question, he answered himself. Gunning down the townsfolk was hardly crowd control. Still, he wondered if he should remove the bullets from his pistol. He set his jaw and decided against that idea. He wasn't afraid, he reasoned, but abdicating his authority was not a solution either. And, in fact, he was afraid.

Gonzalo was not a good sheriff because he was particularly courageous or strong. A few years after this incident he would get into the only full-scale gun battle of his career. He won, but he was glad for the rain that day that hid the fact he had wet his pants. That night he fell asleep crying in Mari's arms. He would fall asleep the same way at the end of this day. Gonzalo was a good sheriff because he was smart and could keep his wits about him even when he was most afraid. And because he cared about the people he served. He cared even about the man he was going to question.

Ferré was older than Gonzalo by about a dozen years, so that they had never played together as children. But Gonzalo had respected Ferré since he came back from the war. For a boy of twelve or so, war had a glamour to it that made it irresistible. When Ferré came home, broken in body and in pain, Gonzalo understood that violence and brutality, the stuff of Hollywood movies, had done this to the youth, made him limp. That summer, Gonzalo did not bring out his plastic rifle and cap guns with the other boys; that summer, he read.

All this Gonzalo thought of until he heard another bottle break and the sound of liquid splashing. He walked to the back of the station house to Ferré's cell, where a hand was stuck through the bars of the window holding a broken rum bottle, pouring its contents onto the floor. Francisco was still sleeping soundly.

Gonzalo opened the cell door just in time to grab the hand that held the bottle. He couldn't see a face. The owner of the hand struggled, twisting the bottle about, cutting Gonzalo deeply. This made him furious. Gonzalo yanked at the arm, pulling the youth, a very short teenager, up to the window bars. The teen stared at him in defiance and pain, and Gonzalo spoke to him loudly, so that all could hear.

"Listen to me, Mario. If you hurt him, I will make sure you spend time in jail. Did you hear me?"

Mario continued staring.

"This prisoner is going to be interrogated, he is going to have a trial, he is going to face justice. Do you understand? Nothing is going to happen to this prisoner. If anything happens to him, I guarantee you it will happen to you. Do you understand?"

Gonzalo shouted this at the boy he held, but it was meant for the entire crowd. Neither the boy nor the crowd seemed to understand Gonzalo. Eyes stared at him with determined resistance. He decided that he would at least take that look from the boy's face.

"Now go home," he said, but before releasing the boy, he gave his arm a tug and twist that made his eyes bulge. Then he let go, and the boy dropped to the ground.

When Gonzalo turned to deal with Ferré, he was glad to see he had awakened.

"Come on," he said, and motioned Francisco to follow him to the front room of the station house.

Knowing there would be people listening at the door, Gonzalo took a small radio from his desk and plugged it in near the door. He turned it on to a station that played American music and had it face the entrance. This, he hoped would muffle his voice and that of his prisoner as they spoke of the night before. Under the door, he could see the shadows of people gathering closely.

From a desk drawer, he offered Francisco a cigarette. Gonzalo didn't smoke, but he knew that smoking often relaxed prisoners into saying a few words more than they had planned to say. Francisco did smoke but, having been arrested many times before, he knew Gonzalo's cigarettes were always stale, packs often sitting in the humidity of the office for a year or more until confessing prisoners finished them, and it was time for a new one.

"No thanks. But if you could tell me what I did to be in jail. . . ."

Gonzalo hesitated a moment. He had been hoping for a full confession from Ferré, though he knew there was a possibility Ferré was too drunk to remember anything.

"Why don't you tell me what you remember from last night?" he asked. He didn't consider that Ferré would hide anything from him or lie.

"I went to Colmado Ruiz last night. I got drunk." There was a tone of incipient remorse in those last few words. Ferré knew that drunkenness was the cause of whatever trouble he had caused the night before.

Gonzalo pulled out a little notepad from his back pocket and flipped it open.

"Collazo says he drove you home from Colmado Ruiz at about twelve or twelve-thirty. Is that right?"

"Yeah. He took me home."

"He says you weren't really drunk then; you walked a straight line to your door. Is that right?"

"Yeah. Well, I had done some drinking at the store."

"About how much, do you know?"

Francisco rolled his eyes back in calculation.

"About five dollars."

Colmado Ruiz sold beer at a quarter per four-ounce plastic cup. Ruiz was a bastard. Everyone in town knew that. His trick with the cups of beer was to charge for a full cup even if half of it was foam. Since he was the one pouring out the beer, half the cup was almost always foam. Five dollars would be something less than four bottles of beer. Expensive, but at Colmado Ruiz you paid for ambiance. In any event, Gonzalo knew that was hardly enough to make Francisco drunk. At most, he had left Colmado Ruiz with a slight buzz.

"Five dollars. Did you do any drinking before you got to the store?" Francisco rolled his eyes back again. This mannerism signified an actual thinking process going on inside Francisco. He was struggling to be precise. This showed Gonzalo that Francisco was hiding nothing. When he lied, he shifted his eyes from side to side.

"No. I worked my land yesterday."

"Really? Doing what?" Gonzalo saw no connection to the case for this question. He was simply interested in anything that might have marked the rehabilitation of Francisco Ferré. At the same time, he knew that while Francisco Ferré working was normally a good sign, what Ferré did the night before could not be excused for any reason.

"I cleared out an acre in the back. I'm going to farm it. It's good for yams."

"What made you feel like farming?"

Without rolling or shifting his eyes, Francisco said, "The girl's going to college soon. I have enough to pay her way, but I want to get her a car. Don't tell her, okay?"

Gonzalo was stunned by the revelation but assured Francisco he would say nothing.

"So, what did you do after Collazo dropped you off?"

"Went inside, got a bottle, dropped off my key, and went back out to drink."

There was no hesitation in what Francisco said, and Gonzalo knew of his routine.

"You drank on your porch?"

"Yeah."

"Did you do any walking? Go anywhere?"

Francisco rolled his eyes.

"I walked into the valley."

Gonzalo wrote in his pad, keeping his eyes on Francisco. He knew that writing in the pad invariably made the prisoner want to explain himself more fully.

"What happened there?"

"Nothing. I don't remember anything."

"What happened to your hands?"

Francisco looked at his hands with their split knuckles and crusted blood. He blinked and opened his eyes wide. It was as though they had just then appeared from nowhere.

"Did you fall?"

This was a trick question on Gonzalo's part. If Ferré had fallen, he would have scraped the palms of his hands, not the knuckles.

Francisco rolled his eyes again.

"I think I punched . . . I think I punched a cow."

"A cow?" Gonzalo asked, scribbling into his notepad.

"A horse?" Ferré countered.

"Where did you find this . . . uh, the . . . animal?"

"That I don't know. In the valley, I know that, but I can't say whose farm it was. Sorry." Ferré was beginning to think the incident with the cow might be important. He was becoming a bit flustered.

"That's all right. I'm just wondering. . . . Are you sure you didn't hit any humans? I mean, are you positive it was an animal?"

Francisco exhaled and vigorously rubbed his face and neck. It was as though the last two questions had exhausted him entirely. He rolled his eyes again and then began to shift them about, searching for answers on the floor. For Gonzalo, this was a telling sign.

"Maybe somebody said something to you, and you beat them up."

Francisco hesitated still.

"I don't think so. . . ."

"But maybe?"

After some hesitation, "Yeah, maybe."

"If you were drunk, could you have hit a woman?"

"Well, if I was drunk, I could have hit anyone, but what woman would be on the street at that time?"

Francisco was becoming defensive, and this was something Gonzalo wanted to avoid. He knew exactly what to suggest to Francisco to disarm him in his growing hostility. He had known Francisco Ferré for many years, had interrogated him many times, and could play with Ferré's emotions as a child might play with sand. This was no special skill; anyone in town would have known what to say to hurt him. In fact, many were waiting to say just those things. In retrospect, it was cruel of Gonzalo to take advantage of his prisoner as he did that day; he would be the first to admit this himself. At the time, however, he was convinced that Ferré was guilty of a heinous sin. More important than Ferré's feelings at the time, were his words. Getting him to talk was all; tears could be wiped away later.

"How about Yolanda? If she got you upset last night, do you think you might have let her have it?"

Gonzalo knew it was cruel to make the suggestion, but he felt the need to push Ferré, to shake him. Had he listened carefully, he might have heard the sound of Francisco Ferré shattering to pieces. Instead, all he heard was Ferré gasping for breath. The man looked at his bloodied hands, stared at them wild-eyed, hated them. Tears began to flow freely and unchecked.

"Did I hurt her?" was all he could ask.

"Would you like to go to the hospital to see?"

Why Gonzalo added that twist to the knife even he could not explain. Part of him regretted the words as he said them. He convinced himself that it was needed; it was like being at a hunt and going in for the kill. He felt certain that Ferré would confess any crime at this point. It did not even occur to him then, that if he confessed to beating his wife, a crime he most certainly did not commit, then his confession to raping his daughter might be equally valueless. There was a smell of blood, and the hunter went for the throat.

"I hurt her?" Francisco repeated.

"Do you remember anything about last night?"

"No."

"Do you remember meeting anyone in the valley?"

"No. Did I hurt her?"

"How about Luisa? Yolanda's not in the hospital. I expect her to come bail you out soon, but Luisa really is in the hospital. Later, I'll take you to see her if you think that will help your memory."

This was clearly too much for Francisco.

"I beat Luisa?" he asked.

"No," Gonzalo said. "Luisa Ferré was beaten and raped last night. The beating was not such a big deal, but . . ."

"I raped her?" Francisco asked.

Now he was beside himself completely. He was a desperate man at that moment. At this point, now that Francisco was on the verge of confession, Gonzalo relented.

"Luisa Ferré was beaten and raped last night. You are the number one suspect. You had said some things about wanting to get a woman to Collazo?"

Ferré couldn't speak for a full minute. He couldn't even breathe. Something inside was strangling him.

Finally, "Yes."

"You were in the area. Your hands say you beat up on someone. Nobody else has any bruises. You were drunk. I know you get a little . . . out of control sometimes when you drink. . . ."

"You're right," was all Francisco could say.

He held his head in his hands and cried with shame and guilt. He would have scratched at his eyes, the tears were so hot, except that Gonzalo was there.

"Do you remember what happened last night?" Gonzalo asked.

Now that he had achieved the confession, now that Francisco had convicted himself, he wished there were another suspect to this crime. But there was none other. In his eyes, all that Francisco said and felt was confirmation of his strongest suspicions. At the moment, he thought the case airtight.

"I don't remember. I know there was a cow somewhere. I'm sure of it. But, really, I don't remember seeing Luisa. Honest to God and the Virgin, I don't remember seeing her last night. I don't remember any sex. Honest, I don't."

"It's all right. It's all right," Gonzalo said. Francisco was becoming anxious.

"But maybe you did . . . attack her, right?"

"Maybe, I don't know. . . . Is she going to be all right?"

"She'll recover. Don't worry about her. She's young."

Gonzalo reached over to put an arm around Francisco. Francisco crumpled under his touch and began to sob into the officer's shirt.

On his part, Gonzalo had to do all he could to keep from shedding tears.

At that moment, Yolanda Ferré knocked at the station house door and announced herself through the keyhole.

At that exact moment, the mayor and Collazo were making their visit with Luisa in the clinic.

As they walked to the door of the clinic, Collazo stopped for a moment and looked up at the sky. It was darkening. Ramirez asked what was the matter in his gruff fashion and Collazo responded.

"Are you sure you want to do this?"

"You're the one asking the questions. How else are we going to build a case?" the mayor responded.

He was right of course. If Luisa had told all she knew of the attack on her of the night before, her father would never have been arrested. The real attackers would have been in custody. Justice would have prevailed on that day. In fact, if Collazo had gone straight to the young lady's room, he might have saved the town some sorrow. But he hesitated with a hesitation that was only human. Had he been able to avoid it, he would have, but no real blame can be laid on him. Not only was his procrastination natural, it was in part an outgrowth of the fact that Ramirez insisted on going with him.

With the bull-headed mayor at his side, he could only foresee disaster from the coming interview, so before heading for Luisa's room, Collazo spoke to her doctor and her nurse. They told him that she was awake and able to speak but warned him against any jarring questions. Since the mayor was there, this warning was destined to be ignored. Collazo then found Mari and spoke with her.

"¿Cómo está la muchacha?" he asked. "How's the girl?"

"She's fine. She'll survive. She's young," Mari answered, but these words sounded foolish to her even as she said them.

"Has she said anything? You know. About the attack."

"No. I haven't even tried to ask. Is that what you came here for?"

"Yup."

Collazo would have liked to have stayed talking with Mari, but Ramirez had already walked into Luisa's room, and there could be nothing worse than to have the poor, abused girl talk to the mayor about this incident. Not that Ramirez wanted to talk to Luisa. He couldn't think of a nice way to put the questions he had, and even he knew they had to be put in a nice way.

Luisa turned her head away from him as he approached.

"What do you want?" she asked.

Ramirez paused a moment at her side, and his throat became knotted. Headstrong as he was, he had a heart, and seeing the girl as she was and knowing he had no help she would want, hurt him. Collazo came to his rescue.

"I think the doctor wants to see you," he told Ramirez in a low voice.

Ramirez left, relieved, and Collazo edged to Luisa's bedside. She turned to him, and he took her hand in his, looking into her eyes. He could not resist the tears forming in his own eyes, and he was old enough not to try. On her part, Luisa liked Collazo. Somewhere she had a picture of him carrying her on his shoulders when she was a toddler. This was something Collazo had long ago forgotten about, but she kept it like the other mementos of her youth—her teddy bears, her school commendations, her communion dress—all these things she stored away, out of sight but safe. She cried also when she saw the old man's tears. They stayed this way, hand in hand and silent for some minutes before either said anything.

"Dime, hija," Collazo said. "Tell me, child."

With that, her story flowed from her. She had been with Carlos the night before. They had been at the car party. Gonzalo had seen them and told them all to go home. All the youths ignored him. She and Carlos left at one in the morning. No, they had only seen Gonzalo once. They went farther toward Comerio; Carlos had left his car at home and would have to walk back. They made love in a field—she wasn't sure whose it was. Yes, probably in Don José's field.

Then what? Then her life fell apart.

"After the . . . the . . . the relations, what happened then?"

Collazo didn't normally speak of such matters with his wife of more than half a century, and he was clearly flustered by having to ask. But this made Luisa more responsive, not less. She appreciated that someone could be embarrassed for her. Somewhere inside her, she knew that her recent behavior had been inappropriate. She knew she had been bad, but she didn't need anyone to blame her as she was sure her parents did; she needed someone to share her guilt as Collazo seemed able to do by simply mentioning the act.

"What happened, my child?"

"We fell asleep. I don't know for how long, maybe an hour. A little more."

"In the field? What about bugs?"

It didn't fit into his mind that anyone would want to lie on the ground for a moment longer than necessary.

"We use bug spray. They don't bother. It keeps all the animals away."

Collazo paused, and Luisa knew what he was thinking. Obviously the spray didn't keep all the animals away from her.

"What happened when you woke up?" He asked.

Luisa began to cry. Her face became red, and her nose was scrunched. Her brow furrowed with the softness of a girl who still retained her baby fat. She wasn't sad so much as furious. Her face was contorted with the confusion of finding a proper channel for her anger. She released Collazo's hand and began pointing at . . . she knew not what. She answered.

"I woke up because he was making noise. When I focused, Carlos was having sex with another girl. He was doing it with her, he was humping that . . . that slut two feet away from me. I heard him because he was in the middle of coming in her. He always makes noise when he comes."

In his many years, Collazo could not recall anyone speaking any plainer to him than this young girl did. He decided her foul language came from stress and anger.

"Then what?" he asked.

She wiped away her tears.

"I got up and tried to pull him off, but she had a friend there. I didn't see her. She attacked me from behind, kicking me. She knocked me down and sat on my back. She kept punching me. Then the other girl, the one Carlos was with, came over too. Her name is Maria. Maria Santiago. I think her friend's name is Minerva, something like that, Minerva Cruz."

Collazo took out a notepad and began writing.

"The one he had relations with was Maria?"

"Yeah."

"The one who kicked you was Minerva?"

"Yeah."

"But you said you didn't see her."

"But they were at the car party together. They came in a little after Gonzalo left."

"Okay. Go on."

"Well, the other one came over, Maria, and they both started to beat me up bad. They're from Comerio, those girls. The girls from Comerio are all whores."

"Okay, but what was Carlos doing at this time? Was he beating you?"

Whatever composure Luisa had gained in telling the story so far began to ebb from her at this question.

"Did he hit you?"

"No."

"Did he try to help you?"

"No."

"Then what? Did he just leave?"

"He watched."

"He . . . just sat there?"

"He took out a cigarette and watched and laughed. He got excited again watching three naked women fighting."

"Minerva was naked too?"

"Yeah. That's how I got away. When she was on top of me, on my back, I reached behind and grabbed her . . . breast. She got off me then, but I wouldn't let go. She punched me in the face, but I didn't let go. I was angry. Then Maria came over with a rock and did this to me."

She raised her broken arm.

"Then you ran away?"

"Yeah. Well, first I fell down. Maria threw the rock at me, and she did this."

She turned and showed a bandage on the back of her head where the doctor had shaved and stitched.

"Then she got another rock and did this."

She turned further and raised her hospital gown to show her right buttock where there was a raised purple welt about six inches in diameter.

"That's when I started to walk away. I started to go home."

"Is that when you started screaming?"

"Screaming? Oh. No. Not exactly." She seemed inclined not to explain any further, but Collazo pressed her.

"Why did you scream?"

"When I had walked away a little, maybe twenty steps or thirty, anyway it was only a minute or two after I started walking, I heard Carlos."

"What did he say?"

"He didn't say anything. . . . He was grunting."

"Grunting?" Collazo asked; then it sank in.

"Minerva?" he asked.

"I guess so. I don't know. Why don't you ask him?" Luisa responded, and Collazo knew the interview was about over.

"You said they live in Comerio?"

"Yeah. I don't know their address. They don't go to school with me," she said. "I'm feeling a little tired now. Could you leave for a while?"

"Sure, sure." Collazo turned to go.

"Luisa."

She looked at him.

"Forget him," Collazo said.

"It's not that easy. It's not."

"Try, child. Try."

With that advice, Collazo went out into the hallway to brief Ramirez.

CHAPTER FOURTEEN

It was in this way that the mystery of the attack on Luisa Ferré was solved. There had been no rape. The broken bones and bruises had been caused by other young girls during a fight. Francisco Ferré was guilty of nothing. Carlos Romero was guilty of many things but little if anything illegal. In fact, as far as Collazo could see, there wasn't even too much point in picking up the two girls who had done the beating. He couldn't imagine that Luisa would want to testify against them in a San Juan court; and without her, there would be no case. At most, the judge would issue a small amount of probation time. Maria and Minerva would miss a day or two of class, no more.

Still, the girls from Comerio had to be picked up. Maybe the humiliation of being taken from their homes in front of their neighbors would serve as some punishment. Before any justice could be done, however, Collazo knew he had to inform Ramirez, who stood in the clinic hallway with Mari.

"How is she?" Mari asked.

"She'll survive."

"What did she say?" Ramirez asked.

"It wasn't her father."

Mari let out a deep sigh as though she had been holding her breath since the screams that night. A tear came down her cheek. Ramirez felt no relief from this news. The thought of having to apologize crossed his mind.

"You sure? She could be protecting him."

"Nope. She's telling the truth. We can let Francisco go."

"We'll keep him until we get a confession from that Romero kid. . . ."

"It wasn't Romero."

"All right, then who?"

"Two girls from Comerio beat her up. Romero just watched."

Ramirez stood for a moment, stunned by the revelation. He wasn't officially in charge of the investigation, but as many in Angustias could testify, that did not stop him from making decisions about how it should be conducted. Gonzalo would normally protest this meddling, but Collazo was not one to refuse his mayor's directions. In this moment, however, as the mayor stood silent, Collazo tried to move away toward the door. He wanted to be gone when Ramirez finally decided what should be done; this way there would be no instructions to follow. Sadly, Ramirez made up his mind before Collazo could get far enough away.

"Go get the girls. Pick up one of Comerio's deputies and bring the girls to the station house."

"Shouldn't I tell Gonzalo?"

"I'll tell him."

With those instructions, Collazo left for Comerio. There would be plenty of deputies at José's farm. It seemed likely to Collazo that any of them would know who these girls were and where they lived. How could it be otherwise? Obviously they were troublemakers, and it was unlikely that this was their first offense. He expected that the short trip into Comerio would clear up everything.

Driving into the valley, he didn't have to reach José's farm to find a deputy from Comerio. Collazo pulled over and asked one of them to accompany him into town. An older man, balding and heavy, got into the car, happy to be out of the heat of the rising sun. He rested his arm on the open door window and drummed on the roof of the car with his fingers. As they entered Comerio, it struck him that he wasn't simply getting a ride home and he began to ask questions.

"Why are we going into town?"

"I have to make an arrest."

"You need me for backup?"

Collazo was twenty years older than his passenger but in prime physical condition for a man his age. He had worked in the fields since childhood and still maintained a small farm, though he worked full-time with Gonzalo. The man next to him did not impress him as being able to provide backup even in the arrest of two teenage girls.

"No. I need directions."

"Oh. Who are we going to get?"

"Two girls that need to be questioned. Maria Santiago and Minerva Cruz. They go to the high school out here."

Collazo pulled up at a stoplight, happy to have a moment to think of what he was going to say to Maria and Minerva. The deputy got out of the car.

"Where are you going?"

"I'm not going to that house. Look. Make a right at the second light. Go two blocks. They live in a red house. It's the only red one on that street; you can't miss it."

"They live together?" Collazo asked.

"You'll see," was the only reply, but the deputy was already running away.

The light changed, and Collazo followed his directions.

The red house on Calle Rio was dirty. There were car parts, weeds, crumpled clothes, broken toys, a rain-washed book, beer cans, and innumerable cigarette butts where a front lawn had once been. As Collazo would find, there was only more dirt inside the house.

After studying the house from his car, Collazo stepped out and began his walk to the front door. He sensed that this arrest might prove more difficult than expected. Just the fact that he would have to take both girls at the same time was a complication he had not foreseen. Still, as he opened the gate he thought arresting two girls could not be so hard.

The opening of the gate attracted the attention of a mangy German shepherd that came running and barking from somewhere behind the house. Collazo drew his weapon and cocked the gun, and the animal, apparently knowing precisely what was the next step, stopped in its tracks and headed off back where it had come from, wincing and whining as though in apology. Collazo kept the gun out as he made his way to the door and knocked. After several tries, he got a reply.

"Nobody home," came through the door.

"I just need to speak to your daughters," Collazo yelled.

"I have no daughters."

This banter through the door might have kept Collazo longer had it not been for the slam of the rear screen door. At this sound Collazo raced around the house to see both young ladies climbing over the rusty chain-link fence that separated their property from that of their neighbors behind. Collazo got over the fence and began a chase of the girls. They were much shorter than he, and his longer legs gave him an advantage. His other advantage was that he was smarter.

The girls looked back as they made it over the next fence. He was gaining on them, but they were confident because they were young. Collazo kept his pace but moved behind slightly to their left.

He hoped they would go to their right and into a patch of hills and woods. Both girls had their hair permed. He equated that with a bourgeois attitude that would mean they were unfit for running through the woods. He assumed that if he could force them into the woods, they would stumble and fall, the race would be over, and the arrests could be easily made. He was right. In part.

"You're gonna have a heart attack old man if you don't stop," one of them yelled to him as they climbed another fence.

Collazo said nothing. He simply made his move to their left even more pronounced.

"Where are you going?" one shouted.

He moved even farther to the left, and they made a dash for the woods as he had hoped.

As soon as Collazo entered the woods, he found the first of his suspects sprawled on the ground clutching her ankle and red in the face. The other girl continued running deeper into the woods, abandoning her companion. Collazo had no doubt, however, that the same fate awaited the runner in the thick undergrowth.

"Are you going to help me?" Maria Santiago asked. "I think I broke my ankle."

Collazo took out his handcuffs.

"Yeah? You think it's broken? Let me see," he said as he cuffed one of her wrists to her injured ankle.

"I think it's just twisted," he said as he ran after Minerva.

In fact, it was broken.

Minerva Cruz proved a little more difficult to subdue. She got much farther but was also stopped by her lack of respect for the nature that surrounded her. It seems that the closest either of these young ladies had ever been to nature was to lie naked in the grass under a sweating young lover.

Minerva got entangled with a thin vine, which unfortunately for her was attached at one end to a nearby coffee tree, home to a small nest of hornets. The ferocious attack of the nest's defenders made her lose her balance so that she slid part of the way down a steep hill, flailing her arms about uselessly. By the time Collazo got to her, she had been stung almost a dozen times. He dragged her up the hill, crying. He was himself stung three times since hornets are notoriously undiscriminating. Collazo, however, had stopped counting the number of times he had been stung by hornets decades earlier.

What hurt a great deal more was that when she had finished flailing at the hornets Minerva began flailing away at him. She badly bruised his arm and bloodied his lip, but he ignored her until she began using her nails. At that point, he pinched her arm in the way he had done to his children when they misbehaved. She let out a yelp but was quiet the rest of the way out of the woods.

By the time he got both girls back to his car, it was well past nine o'clock. Once there, the owner of the house came out, and she demanded an explanation of him. Why was he arresting these innocent young ladies? He said he couldn't say until he had spoken with his sheriff. Then the mother stunned him.

"If it's about last night, it's not their fault. That other girl started. I know everything. It's the word of two against one. Let my girls go, or there'll be trouble."

The stunning part for Collazo was that the girls would dare talk to their mother about their activities and that their mother would not have flogged them to within an inch of their young lives.

"Mire, Señora," he said. "Look, lady. If these are your daughters, you should be taking a little better care of them. You should know what they do at night and stop them. This is no way to give them a good example. This is no way of being a parent." With that, Collazo climbed into his car.

The mother had nothing to say to this. She only smiled at the officer, and when he drove away, she turned back into the house without waving and broke into laughter as he turned the corner. Other young ladies came out of their rooms, one in gym shorts and a bra, one in a see-through teddy, one holding a towel to her chest with nothing else on at all.

It took her a minute to tell the girls what had just happened, and when she ended with Collazo's reprimand she laughed again. The other girls found it funny too, but the one in the towel asked, "Does this mean we have to move again?"

"Let me worry about that," the older woman said. "I'll find us someplace nice."

Collazo wondered about the mother as he fastened his seat belt and drove off. Though she wore fishnet stockings and a short skirt, he could almost swear the woman was his age. Perhaps the wrinkling effects of the sun. Or smoking. Or both.

During the ride into Angustias, Maria was in no mood to do anything but moan and sob alternately. Minerva was silent most of the way, speaking only to heap abuse on Collazo. For his part, Collazo ignored the girl, only looking at her when she asked a direct question.

"So what are you arresting us for? For having sex or for defending ourselves?"

Collazo looked into the rearview mirror at Minerva and noticed the numerous hornet stings on her face. One of her eyes had closed and the tip of her nose had been stung so hard that it was slowly dripping blood. Maria was resting her head on Minerva's shoulder and crying. He looked at them again in his mirror. He guessed their ages to be about fifteen. He wondered for a moment what was happening to the world when girls this young would freely engage in all the activities they were apparently guilty of, talk of these activities with their mother, and resist arrest. He looked into his mirror again and saw two girls, tired and grumpy and in pain, and when the time came for him to turn onto the road to the station house he continued driving straight instead. He would not have done this for any other prisoner, but he thought the girls might be better served if they saw a doctor before jail.

In the clinic parking lot, Collazo honked his horn until the nurse came out. She helped him get the girls out of the car, and as they headed for the clinic entrance, he whispered to her.

"We have to take them to a room as far from the Ferré girl as we can get."

It was about ten o'clock when they entered the building. A crack of thunder could be heard. The sky above was growing a dark shade of gray. The lightning strike was long and thin and so brilliant it left its mark on your mind's eye even after you'd turned away, trying to forget the flash. As the clinic's glass door closed behind him, Collazo took a look back at the storm-choked sky. Instantly, he knew it would begin raining in a few minutes, that the storm would be blinding for a quarter of an hour, maybe less, and that it would then move on, leaving the rest of the day dry and hot.

"Are these the girls?" Ramirez asked.

He had appeared from nowhere it seemed.

"Weren't you going to talk with Gonzalo?" Collazo responded.

"What's the point of talking to him if I haven't even heard what they have to say for themselves?"

"The point is—"

"Forget Gonzalo. He hasn't done a damn thing right so far. Let me talk to them."

With that, the mayor rushed the girls into an examining room. He would interrogate while the doctor saw to their needs.

Collazo knew there would be little point in arguing. As the door closed, he scurried out of the clinic. With any luck, he thought, he could beat the storm to town. We'll leave him for now. The troubles he found in town were great enough. It will be instructive to see what the mayor's interrogation of the girls consisted of.

The doctor began his treatment of the girls by applying an ointment to Minerva's hornet stings to relieve the swelling and lessen her pain. As there was only one doctor, Maria waited in the small room wincing occasionally in pain. Ramirez started by addressing her.

"Did you attack Luisa Ferré last night?"

There was no immediate response.

"Answer me!" he demanded.

Minerva, on the table behind him being treated, decided to go on the offensive even before he turned to her.

"Don't tell him anything, Maria. He's nobody. We get a lawyer."

"I'm the mayor of Angustias. You girls won't get a lawyer until Monday. You better talk to me if you want to be alive then."

Of course, to the doctor this sounded like a terribly empty threat, but at the time Ramirez meant it. He turned his attention back to Maria.

"Well, did you attack her?"

"Go to hell, you fat little turd!" Maria replied.

It was an unkind answer, of course, but in his anger and frustration the mayor did not mind a rudeness contest.

"Is this the foot that hurts?" he asked. "Let me see."

With that, he stooped down and pulled her shoe off brusquely. She screamed in pain, and, hopping out of her seat and onto her good leg, she tore into the flesh of his face with the nails of both hands. He tried to push her back into her chair, but this only brought on scratches to his hands and arms, and he found he would have to leave the room or be stripped to the bone.

In the hallway, the mayor worried. He knew the doctor would tell the truth about everything that happened in the room if there were to be a trial. He would not omit to say that the mayor had removed the shoe of a girl with a broken ankle. The long scratches down his face, therefore, did not represent a crime Maria Santiago could be charged with. He had not been able to get any information out of the girls, and he worried that now Gonzalo would begin to meddle in what Ramirez was beginning to think of as his own investigation. Still, he thought, with so many people in custody, certainly the real criminal was going to face justice.

While the mayor pondered these non-issues and thought they were catastrophic, in town, Collazo found real problems. Though the investigation was nearly complete and the true culprits arrested, the ramifications of that investigation were only then beginning to play themselves out.

CHAPTER FIFTEEN

Rain on a small tropical island like Puerto Rico is often a spectacle. Unlike more temperate zones, rain in the tropics tends to come in sheets. One says sheets rather than buckets because buckets gives an impression of intermittency, but in a tropical storm there is no such thing. Also, the rain can be seen coming down in waves as though the multitude of drops formed a single cloth fluttering in the wind. In this fluttering fashion, a tropical storm can be seen as it makes its way onto shore and from one hill and town to the next.

In a temperate area, in New York, for instance, rain threatens, then starts, then stops. Rain rarely stops in Puerto Rico. Instead it moves on; then you can say, "Ah, if it's raining in Comerio now, soon it will be raining in Aibonito and Yuaco. After that it will rain in Ponce and then go out to sea again." This is how it rains in Puerto Rico. This is how it has always rained here and so it rained on the day of this investigation. As Collazo drove out of the valley and neared town, he could see the rain making its way slowly uphill through his rearview mirror.

As he drove into town, Gonzalo was crossing the plaza headed for Maria Garcia's house. Collazo parked and followed him to the door. Gonzalo was already inside and talking when Collazo knocked. Having gotten a confession from Ferré, Gonzalo was about to release Carlos Romero and ask Maria Garcia for forgiveness. He had gotten her out of bed early for what seemed to be nothing.

Collazo, of course, could not know of Gonzalo's intentions. He knew nothing of Yolanda's visit to the station house, though he knew she could not have successfully bailed out her husband. What Yolanda did do after knocking on the station house door needs to be told before the rest of this story will make sense.

"Gonzalo. Open the door. It is Yolanda Ferré."

Of course, Gonzalo would rather not have opened the door at that moment. Her husband was sobbing in the front room, in the middle of confessing his crimes. But there was no way to keep Yolanda out at this point.

Gonzalo opened the door, and Yolanda stood before him with Doña Carmen at her side. Behind her were a hundred or more silent people. They knew the proper procedure for an angry wife. She was in control of all of them. If she spoke softly, they would be silent to listen. If she screamed and yelled, they would amen her and second her. If she became violent, they would give her room to flail her arms. There was no point in Gonzalo asking the crowd to disperse. This was high drama for the town. They knew lives would be changed after this event, no matter what Yolanda did.

"Can I see my husband?" Yolanda asked quietly.

"Sure," Gonzalo said, and he opened the door wider to let her in.

She took a step into the doorway and stopped there. Gonzalo nodded his head toward the door as a signal to her.

"Come in, so I can close the door," he said.

"I have nothing to hide," she replied.

"Francisco Diego de la Cruz Ferré," she went on, using his entire name. Gonzalo knew nothing good could come of that.

Francisco stood before her as a criminal before a judge. He looked at her with pleading eyes. She turned to Gonzalo.

"Did he do it?" she asked.

"I was just talking to him about it . . ."

"Did he do it?" she insisted, still speaking softly.

What else could Gonzalo say to her? It would not do to lie to her in front of a hundred witnesses. It would not do to lie to her at all.

"I think so. I think he did. I can't think of anyone else who could have done it. He was definitely drunk, and . . ."

"Okay. That's enough," Yolanda said.

Gonzalo wondered for a moment when it was that she came to be in charge of the investigation. No matter. She was in charge at the moment.

"Come here Francisco," she said, and Francisco came to the doorway.

Gonzalo made way for him. He knew that as far as Yolanda was concerned, as far as Francisco was concerned, as far as anybody was concerned, he may as well not be there at all. If Yolanda had pulled out a knife to stab her husband, there would not be much he could do to stop her. The people of Angustias would support her, and he didn't have enough bullets for all of them. On the other hand, if she put out her hand and took Francisco by the arm, they would walk home unmolested by him.

"Did you do it?" she asked her husband. The tone of her voice was different now. There was a tremor in it. Not of fear. Maybe rage seething.

Francisco began to cry.

"Did you?"

"I think so," he replied. "I don't remember. . . ."

"You don't remember?" she asked in fury. "Your own daughter, and you don't remember? Did you beat her? Did you strip her naked? Did you climb on top of her? Don't tell me you don't remember. Did you do it?" she demanded.

Francisco could only cry more in response. She reached out her left hand and touched his wet cheek. He moved his head, seeking out the softness of her fingertips.

"Tell me the truth, Francisco," she whispered. "Tell me if you did it. If you say no, I will believe you. If you say yes, I will forgive you. Not today, but someday. Tell the truth. Did you do it?"

All this, Yolanda said softly. She was in control of her voice again. The tones were soothing. Ferré paused a moment, loving the caresses on his cheek, feeling the warmth of love of his wife.

"Did you?"

"I think so. Yes. I did," he replied softly.

"*¡Mátalo!*" someone in the crowd yelled out. "Kill him!"

She wheeled about on her heel to confront that person. She looked at the faces in the crowd one by one. All of this was a drama, and she knew it, but there wasn't really another way to do this in Angustias.

"She is my daughter," she said. "I am her mother, and he is my husband. This is my problem, and I will handle it in my way."

The crowd murmured in agreement with her. She turned back to Francisco.

"Why, Francisco? Why?" she asked. "Am I not still beautiful? Am I so old? Or is it that she did something to deserve all this? Why would you do this thing against man and nature? Against me and Luisa? Why, Francisco?"

Of course, Francisco had no answer to all of this. He had not in fact done any of this. If he were to have spoken plainly, he would have said that he didn't remember the incident at all. He was as yet unable to imagine such an act fully. But how could he speak so freely when the evidence seemed so certain? After all, there were his bloody hands. After all, there was the indignation of Yolanda Ferré. Why did he do it? He couldn't really come up with a motive.

"I don't know," he said. "I don't know. Maybe it was a spur of the moment thing. Maybe I thought she was someone else. I don't know."

"You don't know?" she asked, the fury in her rising again.

She pointed an index finger in his face for a moment. She was about to accuse him of something, but what could she say?

"You don't know?" she said; then she slapped him.

The slap was a roundhouse slap. Easily avoided, but Francisco wasn't about to run from justice. He took no step back to avoid her hand though Gonzalo stepped back, and the crowd behind her stepped back as well. The sound of the slap was crisp and clear, and Gonzalo thought it would have wakened anyone in town who was still asleep.

She slapped him again and again.

"Toma, pa'que recuerdes," she said. "Take this, to remember."

Then she stopped.

Francisco fell to his knees before her, and raised his handcuffed arms, his fingers knotted in a pose of supplication.

"My God," he said. "My God. I'm so sorry. I'm so sorry. Forgive me," he begged. "What can I do? What can I say? Forgive me. Please," he sobbed.

At that moment, Yolanda Ferré committed the only heartless act anyone had ever heard of her. And who can blame her if she stepped back slowly from this shipwrecked man and raised her hand, raised her index finger, and wagged it slowly in his face. Who can blame her if she, with tears overflowing her eyes, wagged her finger slowly and whispered hoarsely, "No." Who could stand against her if she whispered hoarsely, "Never." Certainly she had descended to a merely human level, but then who has not? Of course, she had descended to the merely human, but think of the great force that had been required to bring her down, to drag her down to this faulty state. And besides. Who is to say she has not paid for her cruelty since then?

This conversation between husband and wife was witnessed by the entire town. For an instant, Gonzalo wondered whether he would have to use his gun. He clearly foresaw that if Yolanda had been so forceful with Francisco, the whole town might feel a right to abuse the prisoner. But there was no such intention in the crowd. If anything, there was a palpable pity felt for Francisco Ferré. After all, if Yolanda Ferré turned her back on you, what greater condemnation could there be?

And that is what she did. She turned her back on Francisco on his knees and walked away, picking her path through a crowd that wouldn't look her in the eye. More than ever it seemed to all that she had something of holiness around her. Possibly no one wanted anything to do with her at that moment because they were afraid she would find out their own sins. Whatever the reason, no one gave her a ride and she walked alone to the clinic to visit with her daughter.

The crowd outside the station house quietly dissipated. There were no more bottles. Gonzalo closed the station house door, but Ferré stayed on his knees, crying, his manacled hands dropped to the ground.

"Come on," Gonzalo said, pulling his prisoner up from the floor. "With a little sleep, you'll feel better." It wasn't true, but it was all Gonzalo had at the moment.

With that, he led the distraught man to the station house cell. He removed the blanket, in case, in his despair, Ferré decided to make other than natural use of it. He then lay Ferré down on the bare mattress, keeping him handcuffed though he couldn't think of a good reason for it.

There were several spectators still at each window, and Gonzalo looked up at them.

"Go on," he said. "Let the man sleep."

But no one moved. They were no longer there for hatred. If any of them killed Ferré at this point, it would have been out of pity.

"Go on. Leave him alone. Let him sleep," Gonzalo asked, but he knew he would have to go outside and disperse this small remnant because they weren't hearing him.

As Gonzalo turned to leave the cell, Ferré reached out and took hold of his pant leg.

"Did I . . . Did I really do all this?" he asked Gonzalo.

Gonzalo kneeled to his reclining level and looked at him. Ferré's eyes were light brown and usually an indication of either his placidity or his troubled mind, but now they seemed deformed to Gonzalo. They had grown red and watery. The capillaries were distended so that they appeared raised somewhat above the surface of the eyeball. Worse, they bulged from his sockets as though he had been holding his breath underwater for much longer than humanly possible. As though he were a drowned man, in fact. They looked at that moment as if they might burst, and it occurred to Gonzalo that his prisoner might suffer a heart attack. But what could he say to this question?

"Did I abuse Luisa? My little flower?" Ferré asked.

"Yes. I think so," Gonzalo said. "But I'll get to the bottom of everything. I'll make sure. Don't worry. Not yet anyway."

Now all of this Gonzalo said in the softest tones he could command, but Ferré understood it all as sharp condemnation. The condemnation was made even harsher as he knew Gonzalo was trying to soften the blow for him.

"All right," he said, letting Gonzalo go.

He turned away to face the wall, and Gonzalo left after locking him in. He would have liked nothing more than to be able to give Ferré information about another suspect, but at the time he had no one else whom he suspected. Having gotten a confession from the prime suspect, what else could he believe but that the man was, lamentably, guilty?

Gonzalo went out to clear the windows for Ferré and allow him to sleep peacefully.

"Come on, people," he said.

He began to push gently on some of them.

"Come on, Jorge. Let the man sleep."

"She slapped him," Jorge replied, shocked.

"Yes. And I know your wife has slapped you a few times," Gonzalo replied.

"But my wife is not Yolanda Ferré," Jorge answered. "I would have thought he would have died. I would have."

"Yolanda Ferré is not God," Gonzalo answered, and with that he gave Jorge a firmer push, and Jorge walked on.

At this point, Gonzalo noticed the darkening clouds.

"Perfect," he thought. "How can I run an investigation in a flood?" he asked himself.

But as he began to cross the plaza to Maria Garcia's house, he thought of the coming rain and looked up to the sky again.

"Maybe it is perfect," he thought. "Maybe it will wash the sin of all of us away once and for all. Maybe we'll be clean if it can only rain hard enough."

The bitterness of the day was beginning to wear on him.

The sheriff of Comerio had by this time come and gone. Molina had walked to Maria Garcia's house with the mayor. He knocked on the door and waited. When Maria opened the door, he asked for her husband, the lawyer.

"I'm the lawyer, and I'm not married," she replied.

This threw Molina off guard. He had heard of Maria Garcia, but he had never seen her. He knew Angustias had a female lawyer, but he had never thought he would have to deal with her. He had dealt with defense lawyers before, but his method was usually to scare them. The idea of an unmarried, female lawyer, however, scared him instead.

"Oh . . . , ah, is Carlos Romero your client?"

"I don't discuss clients with strangers," Maria said.

She closed the door on Molina, and the sheriff of Comerio stood outside her door for a moment trying to think of what tack to take next. He knocked again and Maria answered again.

"What is it?"

"I need to speak to Carlos. I'm the sheriff of Comerio. He knows me. Ask him."

"Okay. Wait here. Your name is?"

"Molina."

With that, she closed the door on him again and approached Carlos.

"Mr. Romero. There's a man outside. Sheriff Molina of Comerio. Does he know you?"

"Molina? Molina knows parts of me that my own mother never saw. Keep him away from me."

This was all Maria needed to hear. She knew nothing of being a criminal defense lawyer, but she knew enough to protect her client at all costs. She went back to the door.

"I'm sorry, sheriff. My client would rather not meet with you. However, if you have any pertinent information, I would be happy to hear it and pass it on."

Maria waited for a reply, but none came. Molina was sure he had no pertinent information to give.

"Tell him . . . Tell him he's gonna hang for this," he said, trying to be tough.

"Señor Molina. I am positive that is not the case. Mr. Romero has not been indicted, he has not been tried, and he has not been sentenced. In any event, hanging is not a possible punishment for any crime committed on this island. If, however, you are trying to intimidate or threaten my client, let me remind you that that behavior is a felony offense in Puerto Rico and carries a maximum penalty of five years in prison along with a fine of up to five thousand dollars."

She waited a moment for a reply.

"If there is nothing further, I'll bid you a good day."

With that, she closed the door and locked it loudly. Then she leaned against it a moment smiling. She was immensely proud of herself and her bluff. She thought the look on Molina's face was priceless, and she began to think for a moment that she could walk into a courtroom with her client in chains and walk out with him at liberty. Then she remembered who her client was, and her hopes were dashed.

She had already spoken to Carlos about his performance during the interrogation.

"Why did you say those things to Gonzalo?" she asked.

"Easy. Luisa got raped, right?"

"Well, I haven't seen her, but I imagine she was really attacked last night. Yes."

"Then if I admit that I had sex with her, he's going to think, 'Wait a minute. This guy wouldn't be admitting this unless it were true the way he says it. He wouldn't say he had sex with her unless that's what really happened.' Now that sheriff thinks I had sex with her, but since I admitted that, he knows I didn't do anything else. You see?"

"No."

"If I raped her, I would have said I didn't have sex with her. I would have said I don't even know her. That's what he's expecting; since I admit to sex, he won't think I raped her. Get it?"

"Yes. Now, don't you think it would have been better to have taken the fifth?"

"What for?"

"Forget it."

There was certain frustration in dealing with a client who would plead the fifth when asked his name, but not when asked about a rape.

Soon after, Molina knocked at the door. Not more than five minutes after Molina had been vanquished, Carlos Romero fell asleep chained to the coffee table. Maria Garcia began working on his defense, scribbling out dramatic retorts on a yellow legal pad.

CHAPTER SIXTEEN

By the time Gonzalo reached Maria Garcia's door, he was really in no mood to do what he was there to do. He had only good news for the suspect he would have liked to have jailed and bad news for the one he wished to God was not guilty. Not that he was going to be setting Carlos Romero free just then. Romero was a swaggering nuisance. He had admitted to having sex with a minor. Gonzalo certainly didn't believe that claim, and he wasn't sure that Romero wasn't a minor himself. Still, it was sufficient evidence to hold him for the weekend. His intention then as he knocked on Maria Garcia's door was to show Romero that he was not the only person who could be a nuisance.

Maria Garcia opened the door and showed Gonzalo in, shushing him. Her client was asleep, his head resting on the sofa's armrest, his arms extended toward the heavy coffee table. In Gonzalo's eyes, he could not have looked like a bigger *manganson*—a big, useless fool.

STEVEN TORRES

"How can I help you, sheriff? As you can see, my client is in no position to speak to you," she whispered.

"Well, I'm not really here to speak to your client, counsel. I'm here to speak with you."

"Oh, what about?" she asked.

A smile was beginning to make its way across her face. Gonzalo's look and tone suggested that he had lost the case. She smelled only good news coming. Of course, she was finding it hard to keep from thinking that Carlos Romero had been lucky to have her as a defender.

"Is it good news?" she asked.

Gonzalo became uneasy. He would have liked to have had nothing but the worst news to report. But if that had been the case, he would not be speaking in hushed tones. He would have come into the room calling to his prisoner loudly, kicking him to wake him, dragging him out of the house and back to the precinct, coffee table and all.

"I suppose you could say that. The focus of our investigation has shifted a bit—"

"My client's off the hook?"

"No. I didn't say that. We've merely changed the focus of our investigation. Your client, in fact, has put himself on the hook. It's just a different hook."

"I don't follow. Is he going to be charged with rape?" she asked.

"Maybe not with rape—"

"With some other crime?"

"If you let me finish, I can tell you exactly what charges are being considered."

He waited for her to nod as a sign that she would be silent for a while at least.

"Your client has admitted to having sex with Luisa Ferré"

"So?"

"Let me finish. Luisa Ferré is a minor."

170

"So is he," Maria blurted out.

"What makes you think that, counsel?"

"Well, they go to school together, don't they?"

"And?"

"And it stands to reason that he's approximately her age."

"All he needs is to have been left back a few grades to make him an adult legally. Having spoken to him, it seems conceivable that he's been left back at least once or twice," Gonzalo explained.

Maria Garcia looked at her still-sleeping client. It seemed to her then that the chances of Carlos Romero having passed through his grades without impediment were slim. She nodded her agreement.

"What do you plan to do?" she asked.

There was in her little sense that she was in an adversarial relationship with the sheriff she was conversing with. Gonzalo was a bit more wary.

"I plan to hold Carlos Romero until I can find out his age."

At this point there was a second knock at the door. Maria excused herself out of the room. Gonzalo heard the voice of his deputy asking for him and left the living room.

"Good," Collazo said as Gonzalo made his appearance.

"We need to talk," Collazo said. Then he headed back out toward the plaza.

Gonzalo followed him. He could see that the skies were beginning to darken directly overhead.

"What happened?" he asked when Collazo had led him a few steps away from Maria Garcia's house.

Collazo looked around, making sure there was no one in earshot.

"I spoke with the girl," he said.

"And?"

"And her father's not guilty."

As soon as Collazo spoke this, Gonzalo knew the information he had gotten from the interrogation had been false and worse than useless. The confession he had gotten from Ferré had been a terrible piece of police work. But for someone with years of experience, for a man so proud of his intelligence, this was a difficult thing to acknowledge readily.

"What do you mean?" He asked.

"I mean the girl says he was definitely not involved."

"Are you sure she's not just covering for him? He is her father."

"Positive. She named names. I've made arrests. He didn't have anything to do with the whole thing."

Gonzalo was not yet quite ready to give up his man.

"But he just confessed. What do you say about that?"

Collazo had nothing to say about that.

"Well? What do you say to that?" Gonzalo insisted.

"He drank a lot last night," was all Collazo had to say.

Gonzalo looked to the stones of the plaza floor for a moment. The stones had been there for two hundred years. They had seen a lot in those centuries, but they had no answers for him.

"She says that Carlos boy saw everything. They had sex, then she got into a fight with two other girls. They beat her bad."

"Why were they fighting? Who started?"

Collazo would have given a lot to avoid telling the story he had been told by Luisa, but there was no way out of it. He told the story in sparse detail while Gonzalo listened, wide-eyed. The idea of three naked young women wrestling in Don José's tall grass was shocking to him. He would have to start a program to get the farmers to keep their grass fields trimmed. Starting with his own.

"You sure she didn't just make this up? I can't believe she had sex with this guy willingly."

"If you had heard her language, you'd believe." Collazo shrugged.

Gonzalo studied the stones again for a moment.

"Okay," he said. "I tell you what. Come with me to talk to this Romero kid. I'll be the bad guy; you be the good guy. When you think I've gone too far, you step in. He'll talk to you then. Meanwhile, just don't let Maria Garcia get in my way. I'm gonna slap him around a little and see what his story is, okay?"

"Yup."

The two officers strode back into Maria Garcia's house and walked past her into the living room.

"What about the deal you were talking about? My client says he can prove he's only seventeen," she said but was ignored.

Gonzalo walked to Romero, who was smiling broadly. In Romero's mind, if all that was needed was some phony proof of age, he could prove he was a toddler. His smile disappeared when he took a good look into Gonzalo's face. It was the look of an officer who was about to beat a defenseless prisoner; a look he had seen before, in Comerio. Before Gonzalo could reach him, Carlos kicked out in self-defense, grazing Gonzalo's thigh. This, of course, only gave Gonzalo a reason to be rough. In a second he had uncuffed and recuffed Romero, this time cuffing one hand in front and one behind with the chain passing between Romero's legs. Carlos jumped to his feet and plopped down onto the sofa again when he found the short chain digging painfully into his crotch and wrists. Sitting was the only painless position.

"What are you doing?" Maria Garcia yelled.

Collazo held her back, not even bothering to look at what Gonzalo was doing. He couldn't imagine that Gonzalo could do anything too harsh to this particular suspect.

"I'm arresting your client for rape. We have proof now," Gonzalo answered.

He was applying his knee to Romero's temple, pressuring it into the armrest. Romero was sure his head would not stand this treatment for long. He became afraid. "I didn't do nothing."

"I know you didn't do nothing!" Gonzalo yelled. "If you had done nothing, you wouldn't be going to jail." He pulled on Romero's thumbs.

"Sheriff Gonzalo. Speak to me! I'm his counselor! I'll have you in court! Leave him alone!" Maria said. She too was becoming afraid.

"We have witnesses!" Gonzalo yelled.

He picked Carlos up off the sofa and threw him against a wall. He kicked the boy's legs out from under him, knocked him on his back, and kneeled on his chest. With both hands he grabbed Romero's face and began knocking it into the ground loudly.

"What witnesses?" Carlos begged. "I didn't do nothing! They're lying."

Gonzalo pulled out his revolver and pointed it in the boy's face. Romero's bladder emptied.

"Sheriff Gonzalo, please!" Maria called out. The case had quickly turned into a nightmare.

"Maria and Minerva saw everything. Luisa says you attacked her. They say you attacked her."

"It's a lie!" Carlos said.

Gonzalo cocked the gun.

"Sheriff! Collazo, stop him!"

"No lie. It all makes sense. There are witnesses. They saw you beat that girl."

"They did it! They did it! I just had sex with her. They beat her up. I swear."

"I don't believe you," Gonzalo said.

"It's true! They did it! You have to believe me!"

"How do you know they beat her?"

"I saw them! I watched the whole thing! I know they did it," Romero said.

He was beginning to calm; the trigger hadn't been pulled yet. Sheriff Molina from Comerio always fired off a round to prove the gun was loaded.

"You watched?" Gonzalo asked, beginning to relent.

"I thought it was funny," Carlos said. He tried to laugh.

"Tell me what happened," Gonzalo insisted.

At this point, Carlos was beginning to feel inclined to make demands. He knew Gonzalo wanted evidence.

"Help me get back on the sofa."

"You want help getting on the sofa? Here we go."

With that, Gonzalo grabbed one of Romero's hands and began to tug him to his feet.

"Okay! Okay! Leave me, leave me!"

Gonzalo dropped him back into his puddle.

"Talk to me, boy. Nice and loud. No lies or you'll be sorry."

"I was there. I saw it all. I didn't do anything."

He flinched as Gonzalo pulled back to begin a backhanded swing.

"From the beginning. Don't leave anything out."

Maria Garcia relaxed in her efforts to help her client. It seemed as though the truth were about to be revealed, and, for the moment, that was more important to her than her client's rights.

"Me and Luisa went to the car party. You saw us. You got into an argument with some guy, I don't know him. The tall guy. You told us to be out of there before you came back. A little later me and Luisa went walking. . . ."

"Where to?"

"More into the valley, toward Comerio. We went into a field. We started kissing. We had sex."

"You forced her."

"No. I swear to God. We've been having sex for months now. She's on the pill. Ask her doctor if you don't believe me."

"Okay. You had sex. Then what?"

"Then we lied down together, and she fell asleep. That's what she always does."

"What did you do?"

"I didn't fall asleep. Whoever heard of falling asleep after sex? I hate that."

"What did you do?"

"When she fell asleep, the other two girls came around."

"Maria and Minerva?"

"Yeah."

"Then?"

"Then we had sex."

"Where?"

"Right there. Next to Luisa."

"Next to her? You weren't afraid she would wake up?" Gonzalo was truly curious.

"She never did before."

"You've done this before?"

"Plenty of times. Almost every Friday night for the last . . . two, three months. Luisa never woke up. She sleeps real heavy."

"So what happened this time?"

"I woke her up."

Of course, Gonzalo had heard from his deputy that Romero's groans had awakened Luisa. Still, he wanted this confession to be as complete as possible.

"How?"

"I . . ."

Carlos paused and looked to his lawyer. Maria Garcia had already decided that it was best for her client to say everything he had to say. She had no doubt but that the entire interrogation was an illegal one. Anything he revealed would be thrown out of court instantly. It was in his best interest for him to reveal everything. Besides, the story engrossed her.

"How?"

"I . . . I told Minerva to wake her."

This was a slight twist for the sheriff.

"Why didn't you do it yourself?"

"I was busy with Maria."

There was a lull in the story. Gonzalo wasn't sure what question to ask next, but he felt certain Romero was holding something back. Getting a truthful answer when you're not sure what the right question is is one of the difficulties every investigator faces. Good investigators find creative ways of getting the information they need. This is what Gonzalo did.

He started by thinking out loud.

"Well. I don't know. I have a girl who's in the hospital with broken bones and bruises. She woke me up at three in the morning, screaming and trying to scratch a breast off. No offense."

The apology was tossed in the direction of Maria Garcia and Collazo. Both thought it was meant for them.

"All of this was because some girl, Minerva, woke her up in the middle of the night. All of this because her jerk of a boyfriend was having sex with another girl. It doesn't seem to add up perfectly. Should I believe this story or is there something missing?" He turned to his prisoner.

"I'm a little undecided about this. Let me show you what I'm gonna do."

Gonzalo broke open his service revolver and took out five of the bullets slowly. He showed the lone bullet in the cylinder to Romero, then snapped the gun shut.

"See that bullet? I'm gonna spin the cylinder around and pull the trigger until . . ."

"Okay! Okay! Look, there's more!"

"I hope so," Gonzalo said, and he spun the cylinder.

"I . . . I wanted to have some fun. I . . . I told Minerva to wake up Luisa . . . special."

"What do you mean?"

"I . . . I told her to . . . play with her . . ."

"Play with her?"

"Sexually. You know . . . suck on a nipple . . ."

"Okay!" Gonzalo said. "I get it."

This final bit of information answered a question for Gonzalo. He now understood why Luisa had been screaming and scratching her breast, why she had hidden so much information for so long.

Gonzalo envisioned a scenario that would lead Luisa to feel ashamed of her breasts. But from his point of view, though the information might explain much, it was relatively useless. This was not the sort of story he could bring before a grand jury, not without destroying the Ferré family. From that moment, he was sure that Carlos, Minerva, and Maria would eventually be free to go.

For almost a full minute, no one in the room had anything to say. Carlos was hoping the interrogation was over. He had seen the bullet in the chamber and was beginning to think Sheriff Molina was much easier to deal with. His lawyer was simply stunned by the information, as was Collazo. Collazo felt at the time that his mind would never be clean again after trying to form the picture of one naked woman playing sexually with another. He could come up with little more than two girls playing jacks in the nude.

Gonzalo was confused for a moment. Somehow, though the idea of Luisa with another woman was alien to him, he believed it. Perhaps its very foreignness helped him to believe. But Gonzalo wondered what question to ask next.

"Why?" is the one he decided on.

"I don't know."

Gonzalo spun the cylinder again, absentmindedly this time, but Romero didn't know that.

"Because I was tired of the girl, of Luisa. I hate her really. She . . . she's too boring for me, but she won't let me go. I'm tired of her. I wanted to make fun of her, *pegarle cuerno,* play her dirty. Rub her face in it. I told Minerva to . . . to play with her, that's all. I wish that girl was out of my life," Carlos said.

Gonzalo began to twirl the gun by its trigger guard, again absentmindedly, but the movement caught Romero's attention.

"Okay! Let me finish. Minerva played with her for a second or two. Luisa woke up . . ."

"And?"

"And I think she liked it. She opened her eyes with Minerva on top of her and she didn't do nothing. She smiled."

"And?"

"And I laughed. When I laughed, it was like she finally realized that I was watching her. She got mad. She started fighting. She started calling Maria and Minerva bad names. . . . "

"Like?"

"She called them whores. It's true, but they didn't like it."

"Maria and Minerva are whores?" Gonzalo was shocked. Carlos realized that this part was really not already known to the sheriff.

"Well, yeah. Mama Inez—"

"Who?"

Carlos became suspicious.

"Didn't you say you had the two girls already?"

"Yeah, we have them."

"Where did you get them?"

"In Comerio."

"Right. In a red house around the corner from the second light, right?"

Gonzalo looked to his deputy, who nodded in return.

"Yeah."

"Well, that's Mama Inez's house."

"Those are her daughters?"

"Daughters? Mama Inez is almost eighty years old. She always has good-looking girls there. This year it's Minerva and Maria and a couple of others. Anyway, Mama Inez owed me some money, so I told her to pay me back a little every *Viernes Social*."

"And the girls are the payment?"

"Yeah."

"Then a fight started, and you watched?"

"Yeah. Luisa started the fight, but those other two girls know what they're doing when it comes to throwing punches."

It would be difficult to explain the emotions of the other three people in the room.

"Don't you feel guilty?" Gonzalo asked.

"About what? I didn't do nothing," was the reply, and Gonzalo only waved his hand in dismissal. There was no way to argue someone into feeling something.

Gonzalo thought for a moment in his position crouched by the prisoner; then he rose to leave, motioning Collazo to come with him.

"Aren't you going to take my client with you?" Maria wanted no more of Carlos, no matter what his rights were. She wanted to be rid of him so she could mop her floor and take another bath after having dealt with such filth.

"I'll be back, counselor."

And with that, Carlos was left on the floor with his hands cuffed front and back, and the two officers left for the air outside.

CHAPTER SEVENTEEN

The good thing about having a deputy, besides having someone to talk to and an extra pair of eyes examining evidence, was the fact that two jobs could be done at once. The only difficulty with this for Gonzalo was the fact that he always insisted on giving himself the hard job. He felt that since he was the person in charge, the person with the highest salary, he should be the one to suffer when there was any suffering to do. In this way, if a drag-racing teenager slammed into a tree, Gonzalo would inform the parents while Collazo or Hector Pareda did the paperwork. This particular task, informing family members of the death of loved ones, was a labor he had done more than two dozen times in his twenty years as sheriff.

The work he gave himself as Collazo and he left Maria Garcia's house was not nearly so bad. He explained the division of labor to his deputy as they crossed the plaza.

"I want you to let Ferré go. Apologize. Let him know it was all a mistake. Tell him everything. Tell him about the people we have in custody."

"He might be angry," Collazo said.

"Let him blow off all the steam he wants. Let him rant and rave. Let him kick the furniture. When he's calm, put him in your car and drive him home. Mind you, don't let him walk, even if he wants to. I don't want him going after those girls or Romero, okay?"

Collazo nodded silently.

"What if he hits me?"

"Believe me, if there's anyone he will want to hit, it will be me."

They passed the fountain at the center of the plaza just as the first big drop of rainwater knocked onto the bill of Collazo's cap. He stopped to look up into the clouds. A few drops began to fall. The sky darkened almost instantly. People who had been waiting at the periphery of the plaza to see the outcome of this case put the morning newspaper over their heads and made a mad dash to their homes. In a minute, the clouds would burst upon the town, and it would not do to be out of doors at that time.

Gonzalo remembered the forecast he had heard just before trying to go to bed the night before, some minutes before the screams that broke the silence of the night. A forty-second day of drought. He looked up, and a drop hit him in an open eye, momentarily blinding him. "Drought, my ass," he thought. The drops were splashing onto the dry stones of the plaza at a quickening rate. It was about ten seconds to the start of the storm.

"Let's go, Collazo. Talk to Ferré. I'm going to the clinic."

"In this rain? What for?" Collazo asked, jogging alongside Gonzalo.

"I've got to explain all this to Yolanda. And to the girl," he replied.

With that, Collazo reached the station house, and Gonzalo got into his car. Just as both the car and the station house doors slammed shut, it began to rain in earnest fury, and the sky turned to a near nighttime darkness.

Gonzalo pulled away from the station house as quickly as he could. It may seem foolish to drive quickly in a downpour, but at the moment it seemed foolish to drive for even a minute longer than he had to. Half of the distance to the clinic would be downhill; the other half was uphill. All of it was a stretch of winding road that was torturous for those drivers who were unaccustomed to the hills of Puerto Rico. On most days, on days without the rain, these roads offered some of the better views on the planet. One could see the ocean from some parts of these roads, though the ocean was a dozen miles away. To give an idea of the beauty of these views is beyond the power of words. Perhaps the word "miraculous" comes closest to explaining the sights. In some places, early in the morning, one can watch as the dew rises from a valley. This vapor will make the mountains seem as though they are sitting on clouds. Magical enough but not the extent of vistas available in Angustias. These mountaintops are seen to float on vapor clouds, but above the mountaintops, one can see the ocean if you sit at the top of one particular hill in Angustias. So imagine this if you can—above the vapor cloud, there is a mountain. Above the mountain, there is an ocean. Above the ocean, there is a blue sky. And in that sky, there are clouds.

Of course, Gonzalo could see none of this as he drove to the clinic. With his wipers working as fast as they could to clear the water off his windshield, he could still only see a few feet in front of the car. In this way, he failed to notice the clinic's speed bump until he came back down into his seat from hitting his head with the car ceiling. It had taken him only seven minutes to reach the clinic. Record time.

The distance from the car to the door of the clinic a few steps away was enough to ensure he became thoroughly drenched. Strangely, as he entered the clinic, he looked off in the distance over the hills behind it and saw sunlight. In another quarter of an hour, that sunlight would be over Angustias.

The first person he saw as he entered the clinic was his own wife. She was sitting in the lobby of the clinic. Mari had been talking to Luisa, consoling her until Yolanda came into the girl's room. Yolanda's first action had been to throw herself on her daughter's neck, crying. Mari knew enough to leave quietly; this was no place or time for strangers.

Mari's sleep had come to an abrupt end with Luisa's screams the night before. She had on only her nightgown and a pair of jeans she had been able to pull on at three in the morning. Her robe, the one that had clothed Luisa, was draped over her shoulders to counteract the air conditioning that poured down from the clinic ceiling intermittently. Sometime since Collazo's visit, she had loosely braided her long brown hair. She rose to meet her husband, but still she looked tired.

"Is she here?" he asked of her.

"Yolanda? Yeah, about five minutes now. I don't think they've stopped crying since she came in."

"Well, can you blame them? It's been a bad night."

"Night? It's almost ten. The whole day is gone in this mess."

Mari was an early riser who preferred to have her household chores done by nine or ten at the latest. This was a trait Gonzalo could admire in her but only from a distance. Early mornings simply were not a good time for him; never were.

"Well, at least the mess isn't as bad as I thought," Gonzalo said. "That's something."

"That's a lot."

"What about the two girls?"

"Minerva was bitten by some hornets," Mari reported. "Ramirez had her tied down with psychiatric restraints. She's handcuffed anyway, but he wanted to make sure. Minerva isn't going anywhere; the doctor is still putting her foot in a cast."

"Where's Ramirez?"

"I don't know. He talked to the girls when they came in, but I went to the bathroom and he left before I could see him."

"Did he get any information?"

"How am I supposed to know? I was in the bathroom."

"Okay, okay. Sorry," Gonzalo said. "Do they know the good news yet?" he asked.

"I didn't tell them anything."

Mari had been a sheriff's wife for sixteen years and knew it wasn't her place to divulge information unless she were told to.

"Good. Let me break it to them."

Gonzalo entered Luisa's room, where her mother was still crying on her. Luisa was also in tears. Neither of them was saying anything. They had been like this since Yolanda arrived. The only thing she had managed to say in her emotion was, *"Tu papá,"* "Your father." She didn't know what else to say. Luisa, of course, did not take these words as an accusation against her father. In her mind the entire sentence was something like, "Your father is too sad to come to the clinic." Or, "Your father is helping Collazo and Gonzalo find the girls who did this."

Gonzalo walked into the room and tried to get Yolanda's attention, but he was ignored. Mother and daughter were going through a ceremony of grief where he had no place. He understood that this part of the ceremony, the release of emotions, would take some time. He watched for a moment as mother and daughter wiped each other's tears. Feeling out of place, he walked back out into the corridor. Mari had moved to the nurse's station. She was on the phone.

"Tell me," she said. "He's talking to them now. . . . Oh, wait a minute. Here he is." She waved to her husband.

"It's Collazo," she said as he took the phone.

"It's me. What's the matter?" Gonzalo said.

"You'd better come over."

"Why? Is there trouble?"

"Yup," his deputy said and hung up.

"What's the matter?" Mari asked.

"How am I supposed to know? Collazo never gives any information. He just said there was trouble. Then he hung up. He does it on purpose."

"Well, maybe you'd better go. Maybe the crowd is getting together."

"Sure. I know. I just wish he'd give me the information when I ask for it," he said as he started to walk away.

"Give them the news, okay? Tell Yolanda alone," he tossed over his shoulder.

"Yup," she answered in her best Collazo voice.

Gonzalo gave her a "I'll get you when we get home" look as he walked out the door.

When Collazo entered the station house, it was already pitch dark inside. He rushed to turn on the lights, but this was a futile gesture. To this day, the electric company in Puerto Rico will occasionally shut down the power in some rural towns during a heavy storm. The official reason why this is done is in case a line is downed in the mountains. Most believe, however, that handling the substations and relays during a storm simply becomes a dicey affair and the electric company workers would rather not deal with the problems it can bring. The station house and all the other buildings in the center of town were on a grid that was shut down several times a year. This was one of those times.

Collazo pulled the flashlight from his belt and started to make his way to the cell in the back. He shined a weak ray of light to the rear, where Ferré was leaning against his cell door.

"I'll be with you in a minute," Collazo yelled out.

Whenever it rained in Angustias, which wasn't too often, buckets had to be placed under both the cell windows. That a good storm might drench the prisoner was another possibility the designers of the station house never considered.

Collazo shuffled to the back, using the flashlight to illuminate his set of keys and his way around Gonzalo's desk at the same time. He would have liked to have killed some time. He knew of Gonzalo's policy of always taking the more difficult assignments to himself. He felt certain that this time the more difficult job was his own. Not that he would have tried to shirk his duty, but he would have rather been anywhere but attending to Ferré.

He picked up a wastepaper basket from the kneehole of Gonzalo's desk. "Did you get wet?" he asked, putting the key into the cell door lock. He swung open the door, but Ferré didn't move out of the way. "Excuse me," he said, nudging Ferré to the side.

He placed the basket under the window to the right. When he turned around, Ferré was swaying gently in the doorway.

"Oh my God," Collazo said.

Then he began the work of bringing Ferré down from where he had hung himself from the bars above the cell door, his toes not more than an inch from the floor. This work took some ten minutes. Ferré was heavy, and the cord that held him would not cut. Collazo did not dare to ask for help from the townspeople. When he had finally gotten Ferré onto the bed, he called the clinic and spoke to Gonzalo as we have seen.

Some ten minutes later, Gonzalo arrived. Not a record. There was no crowd near the station house as he parked in front. They had all gone indoors when the rain came and were inclined to stay in now that it was gone. Once Yolanda had slapped him, there was nothing left to look at in Ferré.

Gonzalo parked and looked up to the clearing sky as he walked to the station house. When he opened the door, the sunlight came in behind him. In the ten minutes it had taken for him to arrive, the storm had ended, the electric company had restored power, and Collazo had not moved from the side of Ferré's bed.

"What's the problem?" Gonzalo asked from the station house door. Collazo said nothing, only stood up. Gonzalo walked to the cell.

"What's the matter?" he asked again.

He surveyed his mute deputy.

"Where's all the blood from?" he asked.

He was growing alarmed. The front of Collazo's uniform shirt was smeared with blood. Never a good sign. Still, Ferré appeared to be in the same place he had left him earlier.

"It came from this," Collazo said.

He held out a metal wire for Gonzalo's inspection. Gonzalo took the hooked end that was proffered to him. It was covered in drying blood. He grimaced and Collazo looked up in the direction of the bars above the cell door. Gonzalo looked up, then down to a small pool of blood. His footprints were in it. Collazo's too.

"He hung himself?" Gonzalo asked about the obvious.

"Yup. Ripped the metal edging off his mattress. Tied it up there, put it around his neck, and stepped off one of these crossbars."

"He hung himself?"

"Yup."

Gonzalo dropped the wire and rushed to Ferré's side.

"Did you call the doctor?"

"Nope."

"Why not?"

"He don't need a doctor. He's dead."

"But to be sure."

"Luis, I got him down from there. I'm positive he's dead."

"But we have to make sure."

Collazo had lived with the death of the prisoner for more than ten minutes now. For Gonzalo, it was still a fresh shock.

"Call the doctor, Collazo," he said, putting his ear to Ferré's chest.

Ferré's shirt was covered in blood. The moment he stepped off one of the crossbars of his cell door, the wire noose, made with the simplest knot, had dug into his neck, tearing open the flesh. Several veins and small arteries had opened behind his ears and under his jaw. He had bled to death at the same time he had the life choked out of him by the noose.

"No pulse, Gonzalo. No breathing. No pupil dilation. Hardly no blood in him either, Gonzalo. I've seen dead before. This is it."

"Just get the doctor, please," Gonzalo said, his voice rising with emotion.

Collazo put his hand on Gonzalo's head and pulled him to his chest.

"Son, you've seen dead before, too. Ferré needs a priest, not a doctor. Let him go," he said.

"I know, Millo. But how could he do this to . . ."

The sheriff stopped himself. Didn't know how to end the thought.

"He wasn't doing it to you, son," Collazo said. "He did this to himself. Look at me. Look at me. He did this to himself and to his wife and to his daughter. Those are the important people now."

"I made a mistake—"

"I know. You're not alone. The whole town thought he was guilty. I thought so too. But forget that mistake. You have work to do. If you want, we can see Yolanda together."

Gonzalo did want, and the two of them broke the news to Yolanda, then to her daughter, then to the mayor. Within the hour, the whole town knew the entire story, from the sex in the tall grass to the suicide in the jail cell. By noon there were phone calls from newspapers in San Juan. An hour later, a TV news van arrived. But no one told the story to anyone from San Juan. What was the point? And, in fact, who did not share in the guilt of this tragedy?

CHAPTER EIGHTEEN

How does a story like this end? The rain came in torrents and stayed for hours. The sheriff was glad no one could tell raindrops from tears. His deputy carried a heavy burden in his heart. That night, when he finally got home, Gonzalo was in no mood to be a father or friend to his family. Not after robbing another family of a good man. The senselessness of it, the poor timing, the . . . What else could be said? What else could be lamented?

Don Francisco Ferré was buried in the church cemetery, and the priest, Father Arturo Perea, performed this ceremony of death. Though Francisco was obviously a suicide, it was thought that he was still laboring under the influence of the tremendous amounts of alcohol he had consumed what was really only a few hours before. Or it was possible that the stress of his situation made him insane. In any event, he was absolved of blame for the final act of his life.

Almost everyone in town signed their names to the twelve funeral parlor guest books that were used. Years later, the people of the town would still debate the validity of their feelings on that fateful day. For an hour or two, every one of these people had known that Francisco was guilty: they had all jumped to the conclusion; they had all borne false witness against their neighbor. Through their decisiveness, they had caused a friend's death. It would be some time before they could be so decisive again. At this time, all had guilt to work off for the death of Francisco Ferré, and attending to the dead man, to his funeral and to his family, was the beginning of penance.

Hundreds followed the hearse to the cemetery, but only Yolanda, Luisa, and Father Perea accompanied the casket to its final resting place. Yolanda cried no tears at the graveside. Alone at home and in the dark, she would cry many tears for months after Francisco's death, but only a few days of this was actually for the tragedy of her husband's life and death. She admits now that most of her sorrow was for herself—for the loss she had suffered and the guilt that burdened her. The aura of saintliness about her keeps most people from taking this admission at face value. They think she is being unduly hard on herself because that's what saints do. In fact, however, she has forgiven herself as God the Father has forgiven her and her neighbors have forgiven her.

Luisa never forgave. She wept bitterly at the graveside, and, for months after, she was deeply depressed. She didn't blame Gonzalo—he was just doing his job in making the arrest, a process her father had gone through many times before. Collazo became a hero to her. If her father had been saved from his fate, it would have been through the information Collazo had collected. That he arrived too late was not his fault. Yolanda, however, has not yet been forgiven. Luisa thought, probably correctly, that the slaps Yolanda gave him were what pushed Francisco over the edge. He could have withstood any punishment but the contemptuous reproach of his wife.

When Francisco had beaten Marrero for his reference to her breast, Luisa had found out and been glad. He was her staunch defender, her *"papi fuerte."* She had meant a great deal to him, and, in her heart, she had always known this. In her eyes, her mother had taken all of this away. If only she had cared to visit the clinic before the station house. The great confusion of that day might have been cleared then with no real harm done to anyone. It is feared now, however, that this rift between mother and daughter will never be healed.

What is there to say about Carlos Romero? He never graduated from high school. He went to work at the Starkist factory in Mayaguez–La Tun, for the minimum wage allowed by law. Sometime after the episode with Luisa Ferré, he settled into a sedentary lifestyle. He died recently, killed by a speeding drunken driver. Carlos was in his Hyundai with one of his four children, and the Ferré incident was far in his past.

The two girls, Minerva and Maria, were put in the custody of the deputies of Comerio. There was no case against them, so they were held for the weekend and taken to San Juan on that Monday. Once there, they were simply told not to go back to Comerio or Angustias again. All evidence indicates that they obeyed this injunction strictly. There was, of course, much more money to be made in San Juan than they were ever going to make in the small hill towns of Puerto Rico.

Mayor Ramirez was particularly unfazed by the events of that day. He went on to be mayor of Angustias several more times, and he is now, finally, retired. When asked about that day, he shrugs. "What are you going to do if no one talks?" he says, and, of course, he's right. In more profound moments, he'll admit that no one was to blame for the events of that day. Usually, however, he blames Gonzalo. If only Gonzalo had been more vigilant with the car parties. If only Gonzalo had been more aggressive in his interrogations. If only Gonzalo had asked for help from Comerio earlier. Et cetera. Some in town suppose he's right about that too, for what it's worth.

Both Collazo and Gonzalo were deeply affected by the suicide of Francisco Ferré. There is ample room for them to second guess themselves, but in the end, they would have had to have been different people to have done things differently. When they think rationally about the happenings of that day, they understand that they had worked hard and conscientiously and that no more could reasonably have been asked of them. But this consoles them not at all.

When the younger deputy, Hector Pareda, came back from New York the next week, both the other officers went on vacations of their own. Collazo used his time to clear the vines and weeds from his property. For him, there was something soothing about being in the fields alone before dawn and working his muscles in the preparation of the soil for planting. Perhaps it is the silence which allows one to concentrate. Perhaps it is the uncomplicated nature of the work. Maybe clearing land and breaking up the clay soil was as familiar to him as an old friend; he had been doing it since he was a boy. It could be that he had grown a bit weary of doing work where the results are not visible; it could be that he wanted to get back to a labor where the fruits were clearly in evidence—he wanted to see, literally see, what he was doing. Or maybe the weeds had grown wild for too long and needed taming.

During this time, Collazo went to church more often than he had and listened to the sermons of the young priest, Diego Gentile. There was a whole series on forgiveness that gave him hope. And he visited with the older priest, Father Perea, even more than was his custom. He explained in great detail all that he had done during the investigation.

"Did I sin in any of this?" he asked once.

"Oh no, my son," Father Perea answered. "You did what any human would have done."

Somehow this was not comforting to Collazo. His fields served only as a distraction, he found. At night a sort of depression would haunt him. He had never thought it before in his long life, but all of a sudden he felt alone.

He sat down with his wife at their kitchen table one evening and began to talk about his own mortality.

"What if I go crazy? What if I try to kill myself? Or maybe in drunkenness. It's a mortal sin."

This was one of the few times in their more than fifty years together that Emilio Collazo had exposed the fears of his heart to his wife, Cristina. She knew this was an important moment, but she was stunned silent. What sort of response could she give to such wild suppositions? She felt that any answer she could give would be a stupid one. Yet the fact that her husband was asking these questions meant he was troubled, and she felt ashamed at not having a weighty answer to give him. She played with the doily she had crocheted herself, moving it from side to side gently with her fingertips.

"What will happen if I lose my mind, Cristina?"

"I don't know. You've had it for so long, I don't think you would start now to lose it," she said.

She concentrated more on the doily.

"But what if?" he worried.

"I'll love you, Millo. Always," she said.

He looked at her for some minutes as she moved the doily. When she finally glanced up at him, she could see in his eyes that she had said the right thing. He reached across the table and touched her hand gently and was able that night to rest calmly for the first time in more than a week. Cristina Collazo stayed at the table a few minutes after he retired. She wondered that her husband was so frail that he needed her reassurance. She had become useful in an entirely new way, but she worried that this might say something of a future where she was the strong one of the two. She put the thought from her mind and went to bed. Collazo was already sleeping soundly, and his heavy breath signaled strength to her. Inexplicably, she had managed to console her man.

For Luis Gonzalo, there was no such comfort. Mari could not give the right answer—he never asked any questions. He thought of this as a pain that was completely his.

For his vacation, Gonzalo took the entire family to Paris. This was their fifth trip. The girls would have rather stayed amongst their friends, but no one complained. They knew this was some sort of healing for their father.

They knew the routine already. In fact, they knew Paris about as well as any other city short of Angustias. All four of them would go to some museum in the morning. At lunchtime, Mari and the girls would visit the surrounding stores, leaving their father sitting on a bench before some painting. They would return to the museum some hours later and find him. Usually, he would be eager to talk of the paintings he had studied, explaining whatever insights he had gained. On this trip, however, he was morose. Museums were normally a type of therapy for Gonzalo, helping to relieve the accumulated stress of a year of work. This time they provided no comfort.

In the Musée D'Orsay, he was found in front of the Ugolino scene, contemplating the statue of the helpless starving father and his children. He stood there for hours, and it seemed as though their torture was his also. He had nothing to say when his family found him, tears welling in his eyes. He didn't respond to their questions. Though they were not interested in art, they tried to get him to go into one of his endless explanations. He said merely, "I'm not hungry. Go to dinner without me. I'm going to the hotel."

In the Louvre, he was drawn to Géricault's painting, *The Raft of the Medusa*. He found a bench from which he could see the painting at an oblique angle and sat. Mari watched him for a while. He stared at the painting, his eyes unwavering, and she was sure he wasn't really seeing what he looked at. A large group of Japanese tourists crowded in front of the painting, but he didn't move. The figures on the canvas impressed themselves onto his mind's eye. They stretched and groped, trying to save themselves and each other. For some, the struggle was clearly a lost cause. One man was already sinking beneath the ocean's surface: no one's fault, just the tragedy that life sometimes is.

Upon their return, he was still on the bench in front of the painting. Again, he had no insights to share. He only wanted rest.

The last major museum on their itinerary was the Palace of Versailles. They started out early in the morning and ate nothing before leaving. The women of the family decided they would have breakfast in the town of Versailles after their train trip. Gonzalo didn't object. He said only that he would eat nothing. He would meet them in the Palace. This sounded like a return to form for him, and his girls readily agreed. They would meet him in the Hall of Mirrors. Of course, they all knew that this would be long after they had finished their breakfast. After they had had a chance to visit every small shop and antique store in town. This didn't bother Gonzalo.

When the time came for their appointment, the women of his family found him in the hall, staring into one of the mirrors.

"Anything interesting there?" Mari asked, sneaking up from behind him. Gonzalo turned around.

"What? In the mirror? No. Nothing interesting. Only imperfections."

This last look at the sheriff of Angustias as he toured the museums of Paris and Versailles and found nothing but tribulations shows him as self-centered. In all of this he seems to feel more sorry for himself than for the true victims of the incidents I described. This is hardly fitting for a hero. There is no excuse for Gonzalo. He was being self-centered. His only saving grace is that he recognized this upon his return to Angustias. Once there, he went back to work, cured of his self-pity and determined to learn from his mistakes and to forgive himself.